All are born human, but all are unable to live human. Being human is divine. I find that humans aren't extinct in the callous, fanatic, and greedy modern world. They keep aloft noble minds and human values, even when they drown in the vast misery. I know they live not only on my Kanoli bank. It's an aesthetic pleasure to give them a rebirth in my pages.

Acknowledgements

Stories in this collection include **An Architectural Dream** published in Kansas City Voices, **Spring Man** in Mythaxis Magazine, **Dayal** in Buckshot Magazine, **Yiyo** in Crimeucopia, **Money Time** in Lumpen, **The New Highway** in Third Estate Art, **Mosquito Coil** in Portmanteau, **Kunjan and Kayami** in Stillpoint Magazine, **Black and White Spectacles**, **Diverse Shades of Insanity**, and **God-man** in The Literary Hatchet.

Contents

On "Being Human"

I first encountered Fabiyas M V in a little outfit called Moon Pigeon Press, which published poems as letters. Moon Pigeon Press operated out of Dallas, Texas, I was in Denver, Colorado, and Fabiyas was in southern India. Denver and southern India are probably about as far from one another climatically, culturally, and geographically as possible.

I encountered Fabiyas's writing again in the Poetry Nook Weekly Contest, where he won several times. We began corresponding, and I am pleased to say that, though having never traveled to India, I now have a better appreciation of life in Kerala, a state in the far southwest of India.

While the stories here are not the poems that brought me into contact with Fabiyas, they contain many poetic phrases. There is the middle-aged woman whose "countenance is like a deadpan mushroom" or "Friday elapsed as a yellow mango leaf fell down."

The stories in this collection, "Being Human", illustrate the closer global experience as well as a strong relationship to a specific region that offers readers an opportunity to step into a distinct place and time.

The stories themselves are snapshots from all walks of life. I imagine Fabiyas moving through Kerala with a story camera, capturing the highs, lows, and so many in between scenes in his words.

Here, in a highly specific region of the world, you will encounter stories of loss, love, hope, fear, deprivation, and redemption, universal to the human experience. Traditional Indian culture butts against modern technology, poverty meets tragedy and generosity, and the fantastic meets scientific explanation. Human relationship is at the core of these stories.

As if mirroring my own relationship to Fabiyas, his story "Yummy World" describes how a young girl meets an older man on the other side of the world through an online game. Though from different worlds, they find commonality online. The stories in this collection call on us to cultivate these

Being Human

global connections while looking out our windows, stepping off our porches, and stretching our hands out to our neighbors too.

As Fabiyas writes in "Being Human" when a character stands up to do the right thing when no one else is willing to, "Humans are not extinct among humans." I can think of no better hope, no better call than to reach in to find our own humanity, a humanity that can transcend borders.

John Reinhart
Brunswick, Maine, USA
Author of Arson, Dig It, Broken Bottle of Time, and other collections.

Being Human

"Dad, what's that sound?" Thanu's curiosity spurts.

"That's a peacock, I think."

"A pretty bird with an unpleasant sound!" Thanu wonders at the Creator's mischief. She walks to the window from bed.

It was yesterday that Thanu and her parents returned to their homeland, under the Vande Bharat Mission, the Indian government's repatriation operation for the expatriates. Thanu's father Sourav is an employee in a cafeteria in Bahrain, the island of coral reefs.

Shrubs and wild climbers flourish outside Sourav's compound wall. Luckily, everything has been kept tidy and in order inside by Sushanti, a part-time maid.

Thanu stands beside the window, listening to the peacock. Holding the window bar, she raises her heels to peep into the shrubs.

Nature is wrapped in tender darkness.

Quite unexpectedly, Thanu screams, startling her parents. A poisonous pain passes through her veins. Her father rushes to the window, leaping out of his tedious rest. "Eek! A snake!" Sourav strands in fright. The snake has coiled the window bar.

Sourav tries to suck venom out of the wound on her dorsal palm, but she stops him, crying.

Velli pats her daughter on her head, then takes her to the bathroom and washes the wound with soap and water.

As time passes, death and gloom grow.

"Please take my daughter to a hospital," Velli's voice wavers under her moist eyes. Unfortunately, the hospital, where antivenin is available, stands thirty kilometers away.

Being Human

What makes the situation worse is that they have been quarantined for fourteen days.

Delay is deadly. Sourav and Velli move to the front yard with their daughter. "SNAKE...HELP...HELP," they yell out to catch the attention of the people around, their voice echoes in the pandemic silence.

Their neighbors including children gather at Sourav's gate. They keep a pandemic distance.

"Stay calm, child! Poisonous snakes are rare here. Maybe, a rat snake bit you," Thanu's uncle's voice dominates the hubbub.

None of the people dares to do the right thing. The coronavirus has built an invisible fence between man and man.

Sourav's tension rises like blood pressure.

Death with a toxic shade spreads on Thanu's visage, increasing her parents' heartbeats.

"Please help me take my daughter to a hospital," Sourav raises his voice again while sinking in the vast helplessness before a crowd.

A smartphone camera gobbles the sad scene.

Now nocturnal creatures announce their presence.

An owl hoots from top of the tall coconut palm standing on the edge of the large pond behind Sourav's house. This hooting is a superstitious signal of an impending doom.

"Her destiny is determined," a wizened man cups his palm around his ear and whispers.

Velli slumps against the gray pillar in the portico.

Sourav holds his daughter close to his heart. Now her countenance is deadpan like a mushroom.

Sourav looks for a friendly face among the crowd, but masks and murk keep their identity concealed.

Thanu is exhausted, begins to nauseate.

"No one to help us?"

Sourav's plea is not in vain this time.

"I'll take her to hospital."

A divine voice? It's like a new shoot appearing among dried leaves. An active man is worthier than a thousand passive men. A hero may sprout anywhere in a society.

Dilish, a burly young man with a virtuous sparkle in eyes, is the owner of that voice. He comes forward. He has put on a white dhoti and a yellow Lacoste T-shirt. His black hair is wet. He was taking an evening bath.

"Where's the snake? Is it still there?" Dilish thinks it'll help the doctor give the apt antivenin if he knows which kind of snake it is.

"You can see it on the window bar." Sourav points toward the bedroom window.

Dilish returns like a rubber ball. "The snake is not there. It might have crept into the darkness. Do you remember its shape, color... Is it a viper or a cobra?" Dilish is ardent.

"Unfortunately, I couldn't identify it in the dim light," Sourav replies.

"Dil, don't touch the girl. She's in quarantine," someone among the crowd gives a cruel warning.

"Hey, mind your business!" with a brown frown, Dilish turns his head and stares at the passive people. He goes on, "Certainly, she's in quarantine. But remember the coronavirus is nothing compared to a deadly snakebite.'

Muting himself, Dilish takes Thanu, supported by Sourav, into his van.

One who helps in need grows a god.

Being Human

Dilish's van opens its eyes with a groan. With Sourav and Thanu in the back seat, the van rushes forward like a cheetah. Whispering holy words, Velli stands in the yard.

Midnight, Dilish lingers before the ICU of Mission Hospital. He, too, is apprehensive like Sourav.

Sourav sits on the floor, leaning against the glass wall of the ICU. Being dog-tired, he dozes soon.

Dilish is snoozing in a steel chair. He gets up, an itch injected by mosquitoes – he smashes one with his palm. Then he gets up with heavy eyelids, looks at his watch. Through the tiny hole in the door, Dilish watches Thanu sleep in the ICU. She moves her legs as if restlessness coming out of her subconscious mind. She has been bundled up in a PPE (Personal Protective Equipment) kit. A middle-aged nurse sits in a chair, keeping Covid-19 distance.

Dilish returns to snooze again in his chair. Dawn has not come out of the womb of darkness yet.

Sourav throws open his eye-shutters. The mist of confusion hides his vision for a few seconds. Then he gets up, puts on his mask and knocks on the door. The nurse in white uniform peeps through the half-open door.

"How's my daughter Thanu?"

"She's perfectly well. The doctor examined her ten minutes before."

"Thank you, sister! Unfortunately, I was asleep."

"The doctor talked to a young man. I think he's your brother."

"Where did he go, sister?"

"Sorry! I don't know," the nurse closes the door.

Sourav takes his mobile to call Dilish. "The person you're trying to call is currently switched off' – it's the recorded voice from Vodafone.

Sourav hurries to the parking area behind the hospital. "I couldn't even thank him." He looks around for Dilish's van, though in vain.

Humans aren't extinct among humans, Sourav muses while walking back.

Spring Man

A ghastly silence prevails in the village after the sunset. Not only Manayur village, the whole country has been locked down to combat the coronavirus.

Hashmi puts on her new white sari with black blossoms. A silk sari cannot alter her body, but it multiplies her charms. She has no way to flit with her cronies, wearing the new dress. She feels a kind of narcissistic admiration before her vanity table.

With a sudden shudder, her gaze strays across the mirror. Being a scorching summer, at least one of her bedroom windows is always open. Through the sari-gap, her crescent stomach reflects in the mirror… and just above this, a pair of strange eyes and a long protruding nose at the window!

Hashmi turns back, shrieking.

Hashmi's brother, a sinewy young man, darts along the dirt road with a bamboo stick in his hand. His friends, and an old man too, from the neighborhood follow him. Flashlights create chinks in the darkness. Forgetting the rules of the lockdown, they search in wells, thickets, the old deserted house… but it's a wild goose chase.

Hashmi's brother comes back, panting. *Yeah… I saw… a dark tall… APPARITION!*

Soon the police come and disperse the crowd. They don't believe Hashmi's brother's words. *An apparition is an illusion, like the moon rabbit.*

They threaten to beat the people unless they return to stay at home.

The next night, ten-year-old Sanu is watching a Malayalam movie on the TV in her living room when someone knocks on the door. Getting up from the sofa, she goes to open the door. No one is waiting outside. Rubbing her eyes, she peers into the darkness.

Being Human

Ten minutes later, Sanu's mother screeches. The door stands open, and her daughter lies unconscious with her legs across the threshold. She carries Sanu from the floor to the sofa, music and the sound of anklets still dancing from the TV.

What's going on there? Sanu's dad, who is trying to cool his body off, squawks from the bathroom.

With tears and fear, Sanu's mother sprinkles water on her girl's face. Sanu remains still, but after what seems a thousand seconds she regains her consciousness. She claims she had seen a thin, Stygian shape, leaping from one areca palm to the next in the grove beside their house.

Next, a child wakes up with sweat on his forehead and around his neck. *Ma... ma... clinking of chains... Spring man passes by...*

All are on pins and needles, even though nobody has reported the spring man's atrocities.

Gradually the police come to suspect that there is some truth in the story about the spring man, spreading through the region like another epidemic. A police officer in khaki uniform warns people about the spring man on TV:

The spring man has supernatural powers. He can run at the speed of a cheetah, and leap easily like a monkey from one tree to another. He is about seven feet high with sooty skin. His visage is unclear, albeit he has two lustrous eyes and a nose like the beak of a black-headed ibis.

Generally, this coastal area throbs with life until midnight or even beyond that. But the restrictions of pandemic time empty roads and streets by nightfall. So the air is apt for the spring man to run wild.

A video goes viral, frightening the rustics: the spring man caught by a CCTV camera. He walks in the street light, carrying something on his shoulders. A lean tall figure. Half-naked.

There are many coolies from Bengal in Manayur village. Being confined to the labor camp, some sleep most of the time, but many of them are restless. The police, under much pressure, take the tallest of them into custody.

Joshu, a security guard of the State Bank of India at Chava, opens the back door of his house to hang his washed uniform on the clothes line in the back yard. Someone is there.

Who's this? Joshu cries.

This stranger is very tall indeed. As black as soot. Long-legged like a giraffe. Only his fiery eyes and enormous nose are visible. He stands near the old well. Just a quick leap, and he lands on top of the house!

Spring man... SPRING MAN!

As Joshu cries aloud, spring man leaps and lands on a branch of the nearest sapodilla. In seconds he disappears into the dark. Joshu is like a statue, frozen in fright.

As usual, the police search in vain.

Next morning, they let off the tallest Bengali from their custody.

A whole lot of people in the area are very superstitious. They readily believe that spring man is a ghostly creature that comes to haunt them from the grave.

Being Human

But there is one dauntless, learned man, who has written two detective novels, in the village. He never hesitates to tell people that all their traditional rituals are nonsensical. He even corrects their concept of god. According to him, God is the one and only invisible, omnipotent, and creative force permeating the whole universe. His fellow men loathe his views.

Unfortunately, his name, Velanji, is little known in the literary world.

Velanji cogitates about the spring man. *What the hell does he gain, frightening people? How could he escape so easily?* Velanji wishes the spring man would come to his house.

Pacing up and down in his study, Velanji rules out the presence of a ghost. *Then who's the mysterious creature? A superman from an unknown planet? No, never.* Velanji is a rationalist to the core. He conjectures that it may be a rowdy boy, or more specifically a young man, bored of the lockdown, who creates the trouble. A drug addict or a maniac.

Or it may be someone playing Blue Whale, an internet game involving a series of tasks that end in suicide. Velanji slumps down in his cane chair under the weight of speculations. His thought-producing machine works on…

And what about the supernatural athleticism? Velanji reads as well as writers, he has heard about the Marvelous Spring Jackboot, which is a rare modern product, and wearing which, one can leap too high and run so fast. Not to be made in these surroundings, but a person might have bought a pair online from some foreign country. Far more plausible than some night monster!

Neglecting his wife's warnings, Velanji sets out with an iron bar in his right hand and a jack knife in the pocket of his pants. He searches high and low for the spring man, but in vain.

The lockdown period is likely to end shortly. Velanji gets up once or twice at night – either to pass urine or drink water. He is a diabetic patient. As usual, he comes out of the bathroom at midnight. It's muggy, may be due to rain clouds, and too uncomfortable to sleep, even under the fan.

Leaves are still outside. Even crickets are silent. Summer rain may come soon. Then a terrible noise breaks the quiet. It's a kind of howling never heard before.

Oh, what's that sound? Velanji looks out of the window, startled. *A wild animal near my house?*

He remains stock-still, while his eyes fumble with the dark night. *What's that shape?* A sudden fear jerks his mind. A figure lurks near the henna shrubs, forty meters away from his windowsill. *Who's that at this time of night?*

Velanji comes downstairs. Without disturbing his family, who are fast asleep, he takes his iron bar and the jack knife, opens the front door silently, and then walks across the grass to the henna shrubs.

Through gaps of the henna twigs, he watches the half-naked figure, in black shorts, sitting on the sugar sand with his legs stretched. He is smoking a cannabis beedi, looking up the sky. Velanji waits, holding his breath. The stranger coughs. A dry cough. Then the moon emerges out of the clouds, unveiling identity of the stranger.

My Gosh! Aap! Velanji whispers softly.

Velanji sees a black burqa, specially altered, *and a pair of uncommon boots*, beside him.

Aha, thinks Velanji.

After tossing the beedi stub, Aap puts on his Spring Jackboots and the burqa. No shirt. Slowly getting up, he walks like a rooster in the moonlight. Velanji follows him stealthily.

Being Human

The infamous Aap is an addict to hashish and arrack. Few people know his original name is Sharaf. Aap came to Manayur with his uncle at the age of five. His parents in the neighboring state of Tamil Nadu had been killed in a communal riot. His widower uncle was a mason.

The unexpected demise of his uncle, when Aap was in the tenth standard at Govt High School Manathala, rocked the boat. Aap had to leave school to keep his head above water. He became an apprentice in an automobile workshop, but before long he was trapped in the bad company of the village. His hut on the bank of Kanoli canal became the evil hub of the village, where he and his delinquent friends gambled, watched porn videos, jacked up...

Opening a wooden gate, Aap enters the front yard of an auto rickshaw driver's house. He rings the doorbell, rousing the driver and his family from their sound sleep. Just before the door opens, Aap darts back to the gate.

Which is when Velanji, who is hiding behind the nearby coconut palm, comes forward with enthusiastic pace and strikes him a heavy blow on the head with the iron bar in his hand. The spring man falls down with a thud.

Good afternoon, friends! the Circle Inspector of Police begins his speech. *We've gathered here to honor our hero, Velanji.*

Maniacs and drug addicts are everywhere in the modern world. At any time, they may come through layers of darkness. They are fond of fantasy, insane adventures and sadistic pleasures. These antisocial elements are cancerous in our society. We, the Police, are sometimes helpless. Today's world needs valiant men like Velanji...

Velanji sits on the dais with pride as huge as the Himalayas. *Ways of honor are diverse, and it often comes out of the blue,* he muses and smiles at the audience.

He always cherished the dream of winning a literary award. But even if he won the Man Booker Prize, he wouldn't get this much applause from his fellow men, who rarely read books.

An Architectural Dream

Charming girls, who chit-chat beneath a jackfruit tree in front of the college, magnetize him. A security guard cannot stop Joffin's mind entering the fenced campus. "Look straight, idiot!" An old peppery pedestrian's loud cry startles Joffin. It's a crowded sidewalk. He has trampled the bare foot of the fragile man while strolling with his eyes cast on the girls. The Kerala College of Architecture, with its antique buildings, stands in the heart of the city.

An embryo of an architectural dream begins to form in Joffin's mind. He wants to take a degree in architecture, studying in the Kerala College of Architecture. Education has become too expensive. So even if he passes the Architecture Entrance Test, he cannot flutter into his dream. He should pay an arm and a leg as course fee.

An alarm clock crows like a cock. Joffin rubs open the shutter of a bright day. He has burnt the midnight oil. He takes a quick bath to remove the scum of fatigue. His brown body shares the fragrance of Chandrika, an Ayurvedic soap. He has heard that Ayurvedic soap can erase the fungal infection called 'tinea versicolor' on the skin. Besides, he has no money to visit a dermatologist.

Bell rings to begin the entrance exam. Students occupy wooden benches. Joffin softly reads his neighboring student's name 'Nidha', printed on her Admission Ticket. His fingers move through his architectural dream.

Knowingly or unknowingly, his elbow touches her fleshy left arm frequently, which has been laid on the desk like a bridge. It is distinct through her vague smile that she enjoys this masculine tickle. What makes her presence alluring is the traditional smell of coconut oil, heated with herbs, from her hair. Nowadays, girls at her age apply some exotic shampoo.

A dozen minutes remain to the end of the architecture entrance test. Joffin nauseates. Waves of acidity attack him. He puts his pen down.

"What happened?" Nidha looks at him, and then stretches her water bottle. Water can relieve his stress.

Being Human

Joffin comes home dog-tired. Hunger conquers all other feelings. He can swallow a hippopotamus now. His mother has prepared his favorite black oyster fry. After lunch, he enjoys a siesta on the tattered sofa bed in the parlor, exposed to the wind from an old table fan. He wakes up after three hours, mistaking the dusk for the next dawn. Enchanting smell of the coconut oil heated with herbs and Nidha's soft arm still lingering in his soul.

It will take a few months before the entrance test result comes in. Joffin spends his time in boredom. To save himself from drowning in despair, he reads the book, Wooden Architecture of Kerala.

A sunny morning, Joffin has been installed in the chancel with a flute. The vaulted ceiling of the church always enthralls him. Soon he begins to play his flute. He is a popular flutist in his parish. His mind is receptive to two things – architecture and music. He has many fans in the parish, especially girls. But he is so shy that he hastens to get away from their presence.

Monday is Joffin's birthday. Evening breeze blows. Bats flutter, waking up from their acrobatic sleep in the breadfruit tree. A melancholic tune flows from Joffin's flute. He tries to tame his distress with tunes from his flute. The entrance test result has taken all Joffin's joy away. His mother is accustomed to similar tunes. She makes out her son's failure in the entrance test turns his mind turbulent, comes to the windowsill of the parlor with a cup of steaming milk tea.

"Don't worry, dear. After all, that was your first attempt." She tries to comfort him. Was she well off, she would have definitely paid him to go to the Arch Academy, a prestigious institute for the entrance coaching. Joffin goes on playing his flute. Putting the tea cup beside him on the windowsill, she goes out to the cow-house, where she has housed two cows. Cows are like Gods to her. Her livelihood depends on cows. She kisses on a cow's cheek. They communicate through the lingua franca of silence. Her cow milk is in high demand. She never diddles people out of the quality of the milk, adding water to increase the quantity.

The Arch Academy is a popular coaching centre in the city, like a kind of factory producing the Top Rankers. Though the fee structure is very high, the academy provides free coaching with ten students every year, who are selected on the basis of a written test and an interview.

Now that Joffin has passed the written test after some months of study, he appears for the interview.

'How smart they are!' – Joffin muses, running his eyes over the other candidates around. Shyness makes him nervous and changes the natural hue of his countenance.

The interview board consists of three members, the director of the Arch Academy and the subject-matter experts. The two experts begin to shoot questions. Joffin withstands them with brilliant answers. Now it's the director's turn.

"Why don't you take admission directly, paying the fee?"

Joffin portrays his poverty through pure words. His father divorced his mother, when he was in a cloth cradle. Cow milk has been the sole source of their family's income. He feels that talking about poverty is like splattering himself with mud. Soon he expresses his passion for music.

"Why don't you earn with your flute?"

"I am God's musician. I can't sell music for the material gain."

"Nonsense!" The director is an atheist. He makes fun of Joffin's belief. He resists the director's prickly words with patience.

5 P.M.

The air is suffused with tunes of frustration. Joffin tries to save himself from drowning in disappointment. His mother stops kneading wheat flour into soft dough, washes her hands under a tarnished brass tap in the kitchen, dries them with the end of her sari, and then comes to Joffin with the newspaper, in which there is an advertisement about an architectural contest:

of
m.
ot

people come seeking his blessings.

BECOME AN ARCHITECT

A competition for students with an apti-
tude for architecture

FREE ENTRY

Prize: Cash & Free Entrance Coaching at
the Arch Academy.

*Anyone aged below twenty can apply
online to: arcacademy@gmail.com*

Thanma, a young married woman from

Joffin sits stooping with his eyes stranded in the advertisement. A fresh hope sprouts in his mind.

A cloudy day after a fortnight, Joffin gets up too late. He has slept like a buffalo through the monsoon chill. Soon he cogitates about the big contest at the Arch Academy today. Taking a toothbrush, a tiny tube of Colgate paste and a blue bath towel, he goes to the pond located in the south west of his house, while his mother prepares 'Chammanthi[1]', grinding the grated coconut along with green chilies, shallots, ginger, tamarind, sliced raw mango and salt. After taking rice porridge with the spicy accompaniment of Chammanthi, he sets out to the Arc Academy.

Quite surprisingly, the same director – who had insulted Joffin on grounds of his religion – judges the contest.

"Marvelous!" The director utters his delight and surprise at Joffin's innovative architectural designs and ideas. His architectural excellence

---

[1] *A kind of chutney, which is made, grinding the grated coconut along with green chilies, shallots, ginger, tamarind, sliced raw mango and salt.*

brings him to the velvet chair of victory. Loud applause. He walks into the limelight. The director, concealing his guilty conscience, congratulates Joffin. "A genius weaves his own wings and flies higher than the Mars."

Joffin's monotonous days transform at the Arc Academy. He is a zealous student. His teachers polish and enrich his mind. *What you do with true passion is the real action* – he often remembers his mother's words.

Next monsoon. After the flooding.

"Why are you so late? It's time to close this year's admission." The principal of the Kerala College of Architecture is impatient.

Joffin is silent. "Sir…I don't join B.Arch."

"Why? What do you mean, Joffin?"

The principal gapes at the academic brilliance of Joffin, who has won the first rank in the entrance test.

"I have little money to pay the course fee."

The principal is in a quandary. Moving the glass paper weight on his table, he gazes at the certificates again. Uncertainly, he turns right, and then left in his black Leatherette Office Arm chair. After a long pause, his thought-machine works again, producing words.

"I can help you, my boy. I'll pay this year's fee for you."

The principal's compassionate offer helps Joffin come out of the mare's nest. In his exaltation, Joffin kisses the principal's hand.

It's Joffin's first day at the Kerala College of Architecture.

'Nidha!'

Joffin had just an hour-long acquaintance with her, yet he recognizes her in the campus. Her hair still emits the same enchanting smell of coconut oil heated with herbs. An unexpected smile from her lips creates ripples of unearthly vibes in his mind. Joffin spends his first year at the Kerala College of Architecture – dreaming, drawing, designing and discussing. Finally, parching summer comes with exams. He plows his textbooks until midnight. His flute is mute now.

After the exam, his college closes for the midsummer vacation. Future begins to perturb him again.

"How'll I pay the fee next year?"

"Live now, my son." Experience has taught his mother practical wisdom.

Season of steady rain comes again. Joffin's dream drenches in anxiety. Flute produces tunes of frustration again. The principal's compassion runs out. Joffin gets notice to pay the fee within a fortnight. Night is wet with silent tears.

> *Ma, I'm leaving my college, you and all other precious things. I know we've no way to pay the fee. I'll go to the faraway Mumbai, the city of opportunities. I don't think it will be difficult to get a job there.*
>
> *Don't cry, please! Live with the cows, ma. You can see me in their innocent eyes. One dream can lead us into another. I'll certainly come back with sacks of money one day. Our next generation must never weep.*
>
> *Hugs, Joffin*

Night rain starts. Joffin's mother leans back in her bed with a heavy heart. She takes her Smartphone to reduce anguish, but in vain. His last written words burn in the hearth of her heart. Suddenly, she seems to see him through the blur of rain drops on the windowpane. Petrified, she rubs her eyes. Nothing is there. Now she hears a stray dog barking in the distance.

The Snakeheads

As Rins opens his upstairs bedroom window, the first sight is that of what people call 'hyacinth pond', which is large in size and rather oblong in shape. Now the hyacinths with entrancing violet blooms grow only in the middle of the pond. Monsoon water brings fishes like snakehead and climbing perch into the pond, connecting it with the nearby fields and canal.

Now that the steady rain ceases, Rins walks to the verge of the pond, his favorite hang-out. The sun comes out, unzipping the cloudy time.

"Oh, it's wonderful!" He likes the glossy snakehead resembling a tiny helicopter at first glance. There's enough space for a friend in his mind. Several newcomers have entered the pond in his absence during the heavy rain, he muses.

"My Gosh! What's this?" A shoal of snakehead fry. It's as if red ink poured into the water. The mother fish is also with them. He surmises that the snakehead that caught his eyes first is the father fish.

A breeze blows through fresh sunshine. Rins finds true charms in the nature. Sweet vibe fills his mind. He wants to undress and swim in the pellucid water like a nude fish, free from the artificiality and sophistication of the modern life.

"Rins, what are you doing there? Your breakfast is ready."

"I'm coming, Ma."

It's time to go to school, which is a monotonous monarchy for him. His mother has prepared dosa and chutney for breakfast. How can he go to school, leaving the fish world? He fills his mouth with bits of dosa, some chutney, and water, and then pretends to vomit.

Hearing Rins retch, his mother stops shredding cabbage and hurries to him from the kitchen.

"What happened, son?" Rins is silent, feigning fatigue.

Being Human

His grandmother comes, chewing betel. She spits into a brass spittoon in her hand, and then says, "Rins is very tired. You had better not send him to school today." She pats him on his nape. He feels relieved of his school tension.

Rins lies in his bed, pondering about his classmates, who are likely to yawn or sigh in the mathematics class. Of course, a few of them are studious, and may be gazing at the teacher as cranes at fish.

His mother frequently inquires after him. "I'm Okay, Ma," he repeats.

Quickly finishing her domestic duties, his mother goes to buy broken rice from the nearest grocery. He looks for his grandma. Finding her snooze in the recliner, he saunters to the verge of the pond.

To his dismay, he cannot see the snakeheads and their red fry. He installs himself on the grey granite stone on the edge of the pond. The newly bloomed hyacinths enthrall him.

Soon a 'chip-chip' sound falls into his ears. He looks up and spots an Indian palm squirrel on the top branch of the jackfruit tree on the opposite edge of the pond. Three white stripes which run from its head to grey bushy tail are a paradigm of the invisible creator's artistry.

Rins spots ripples near the opposite edge of the pond. Getting up from the stone, he walks to the green *communist pacha*[2] shrub. To his delight, he finds the snakehead family. They are cozy under the *communist pacha* stems hanging over the water.

"Where're you, Rins?" Startled by his mother's piercing call, he darts back to his house.

As an angry statue, his mother is standing on the threshold.

"Did you vomit again?"

---

[2] *A multi-stemmed shrub.*

22

"No, Ma. I'm okay now."

"If you stand there, exposed to the parching rays, you'll get a fever too. Then you'll be happier.'

Climate has changed like generation. It's not sunlight, but sun-fire. Yet Rins remains perky under the sun. True passion in what he does is an umbrella against sweltering rays.

There were plenty of ponds in his village. This one, too, will be buried soon.

Rins is to face the music, for his mother has made out his truancy. She chides him for his laziness, and describes his classmates in colorful words. Unlike Rins, they are brainy and diligent, she declares. Her visage is reddish dark with fury. His mother is unaware of the real difference between him and them. He's *human*, learning from nature, whereas they are *electronic*.

Rins' school remains closed over the weekend. He wakes up early in the morning and opens the window into the sweet rhythms and solace of the nature. The dawn wind, chirps of sun birds… Such divine delights are unknown to the other children, who have trapped their minds in the electronic games like Subway Surfers.

Rins detects a stranger near the pond. *Who's that?* He runs down the stairs, and reaches the verge of the pond in a jiffy. A pot-bellied man stands, screwing his dark handlebar moustache with his left thumb and forefinger. He keeps his right arm stretched; there is a rod in his hand. He has already thrown the fish-hook with a live bait, a tiny frog, into the pond.

"Uncle, what are you doing?"

"Keep quiet, boy". The angler is a middle-aged man with the skin color of an elephant.

The frog, with the hook put through one of its legs, keeps afloat near the snakehead fry. The keen-eyed father fish, anxious about the safety of his babies, lunges and swallows the frog. As the angler pulls his line, Rins grimaces.

Being Human

"HEY UNCLE... Never be so cruel. Drop the fish into the water, please!"

"Hello boy, this pond is not your dad's."

As the delighted angler leaves, putting the snakehead into his bamboo basket, Rins stands helpless, turning to jelly. What can a twelve-year-old boy do against the cruelty of a bear-like man? Liquid pain blurs his vision. The depth of departure depends on intimacy.

What is more agonizing is the sight of the mother fish looking for its mate in vain. Her beloved's valorous sacrifice is for the family. He attacked the frog, thinking that the frog would catch his little ones.

Next noon, Rins ambles down to the pond with some boiled rice in his hand. The pond looks like a house, where an unexpected murder has taken place. His eyes roam around. The distant rain tree with the deep red blooms seems to burn with the nature's anger. Then he throws the boiled rice into the water to be seen by the mother fish. Though she stares at the sinking rice, she nears not to take it.

Rins strolls around the field, where the smell of mud and paddy fragrance lingers entwined. The nature is a sanctuary of peace for him. He stoops to pick a kingfisher feather. *Soft. Beautiful!* He pockets it. His trouser pocket is full of similar precious things, and looks like a pregnant fish. *The old sun is no more, it's a desert sun that burns in his God's Own Country* – he cogitates about the sunlight while walking back to his house.

After lunch, Rins is sleeping like a rabbit. Screeches of an Indian myna wake him up. Quickly he opens his bedroom window. The myna is on the branch of the drumstick tree in the yard. Rins looks down. Shudders. A rat snake creeps under the tree.

Like a mongoose, Rins darts out. Keeping distance, he watches the snake slowly zigzagging away.

Now what petrifies him more is the angler walking away from the pond. The bamboo basket sways over his shoulders. Rins rushes to the edge of the pond...and sadly spots the orphaned fry. Fuelled by rage and pang, he stoops to pick a stone to pelt at the angler from behind, but he can't.

The snakehead couple swims down Rins' memory lane. As the guardian of the fry, he hangs out by the pond. While watching them feed on the breast of the pond, fresh joys appear like the water hyacinth blooms.

Beyond the Familial Rhythms

His smartphone screen is wet with the lascivious saliva. What an alluring complexion! Her nose fuels temptation. Again, he stares fixedly at her WhatsApp image.

I think you sent it to me by mistake? Saleij messages her.

No, Thanma replies. Saleij is utterly dumbfounded. Though his neighbor, he hasn't any word or eye contact with her until now.

What do you mean? Saleij writes.

What is wrong with the pic? Isn't it beautiful? Thanma adds a smiley emoji too.

Perhaps, Thanma has secretly observed Saleij's family life. Now that his wife is away with her mother, he has been alone in the house for a couple of years. She surmises that there is some issue between Saleij and his spouse.

Why did she send me her pic? What does she want? Saleij is wakeful in his bed, pricked by questions. When his wife was with him, hugged him, he used to sleep comfortably. A pillow can never be a substitute for wife.

Saleij falls asleep in the ash of thought at the tail of night.

Sipping black tea, he checks WhatsApp. Thanma has sent him a video clip. Quickly, Saleij opens the animated video. A peacock spreads its feathers, when a peahen raises its head slowly in coyness. He examines when she sent him the video, and wonders how early she wakes up. The erotic emotion stands erect in the early morning.

Saleij attempts to tame his prancing mind. Down deep, he loves his spouse and son, though they are not with him. She regularly calls him, expressing love and concern. His mother-in-law is the villainess, who is stiff-necked and possessive, and who wants her daughter to live with her always. She had impelled Saleij to stay in her house, but he turned down her proposal politely.

Being Human

He is sitting in his front yard, exposed to the ethereal charms of moonlight. The fragrance of ylang-ylang flowers floats in the wind, the perfume of the earth delights his olfactory organ.

Now a new WhatsApp video comes from Thanma. She sings a Malayalam song, a fusion of romance and frustration. What a sweet voice!

Her music video is followed by a string of romantic emojis. Saleij perceives her true feelings, her amorous mind emerging.

He is in a quandary – between his wife's and lover's love. A cyclone forms in the bay of his life.

If he lets Thanma's love grow in his heart, he will lose wife. Since he lives in an orthodox society, he will have to experience a horrible disgrace. Besides, he will lose his decades-old social status. How can such a disgraceful teacher face his students? He is on the skids. His son's words and voice dominate his memory lane.

Saleij wipes his broad forehead and neck with a blue handkerchief, drinks water from a clay jug. He cogitates about morality and social status, ultimately reaching the conclusion that both are man-made hypocrisies. People without dual faces are rare in his society.

Thanma is his neighbor's wife – a neighbor, who is more than a neighbor. He respects Saleij as his son's teacher and loves him as his friendly neighbor. Yet Saleij is on the verge of falling into the abyss of temptation, breaking all barriers.

Saleij finds a new image, a lovey-dovey close-up of a man kissing his lady, sent by Thanma. His passion unfolds like an umbrella.

Thanma's better half is a nice-looking fellow, Indian white skinned. Unfortunately, liquor has turned his eyes reddish. Likewise, smoking has stained his lips.

Why does Thanma turn to Saleij? Maybe, her husband's romantic veins have lost power. He creates a fantasy world with drugs, sprawls there always.

Thanma loses her feminine charms and fragrance in the wilderness of life. She looks for a butterfly or a sunbird. She doesn't like honey to be wasted.

I wish you could take me to the Nelliyampathy Hills, want to enjoy the green valley from within the lock of your brawny arms. Thanma inserts a dozen red heart emojis in her WhatsApp message.

Pull of the erotic ecstasy is vehement, yet Saleij tries to be loyal to his wife. He knows well that roots of an illicit relationship can crack the basement of a family.

Saleij wants to talk to someone, to unfold his mind, in order to escape from the dungeon of the emotional conflicts.

Though he doesn't give any reply, he goes through the message again. *I wish you could take me to the Nelliyampathy Hills, want to enjoy the green valley from within the lock of your brawny arms.* Maybe, it's not love, but lust is the mortise that joins them; he muses and gives a hiccup.

Next afternoon, Saleij meets his friend, who is a priest in the distant village. He opens his mind before the priest, tells him how Thanma seduces him, sending pictures, videos and messages. The priest foresees the imminent doom; the families of both Saleij and Thanma will be ruined.

"If you bring Thanma here, I'll talk to her. Sometimes a good counsel produces a miraculous result."

"I'll make an attempt to bring her here. Thank you!"

Saleij returns home before the gloaming. He is much relieved of tension, replies *Yes* to Thanna's previous message.

Thank you, dear! Thanma's delight is boundless now.

What do you tell your husband?

I'll tell him I'm going to the shrine.

Okay, Thanma, let's go tomorrow. Wait for me at our bus stop. I'll pick you at 10 A.M.

Being Human

It's a cloudy morning. Another cyclone is likely to touch the Kerala coast by midnight. Neither Saleij nor Thanma is worried about the impending cyclone and rain. His car runs straight; his mind slips out of the steering frequently. Thanma's tongue drizzles romance. As she puts her hand on his thigh, the car zigzags, seems to hit a pedestrian. A narrow escape! The pedestrian turns peppery, pelting obscene words at Saleij, who drives away without stopping.

"Why did you bring me here?," Thanma wonders.

"Don't worry, Thanma! Let's have the blessings of a great priest before we continue our journey."

The priest is a voracious reader with sunken eyes and silver hair. Unlike the hypocritical holy men, he utters words of practical wisdom. Thanma cannot but listen to him. She nods, as though realizing her follies.

She sits in the rear seat of the car on the return journey, keeping silent. Saleij too shares the silence.

"Thanks for opening my eyes!" She walks away without turning back.

Her messages cease to haunt Saleij. As weeks pass by, the root of lust gets dry in his mind. Now his sky is white with serenity.

Saleij is sitting in the portico. Suddenly, he is astounded at the sight – a crowd forming around Thanma's house. He darts to her yard like a bat out of hell. *Why did she do this?* people whisper. Thanma's husband stands, leaning against a pillar. Gloomy. Forlorn. Nobody dares or tries to console him.

Thanma has eloped with a middle-aged Don Juan. A dark, bear-like man. A coconut palm climber residing in her neighborhood. His mind soaks in toddy every evening. Saleij wonders how she could go with such a man. Love is just a carnal game for him. He chats, only to cheat. His motto is: *Throw away after use.* It's definite that he will jettison Thanma somehow.

Saleij's school closes for the midsummer vacation. His wife and son have come home for holidaying.

He wakes up too late in the morning, and then spends his time on Facebook, which becomes his favorite hangout.

Suddenly his eyes strand on a Facebook post. He reads the title of the news clipping – *A Woman dies of Snakebite.* Thanma's photo also appears on the page.

Saleij is down in the dumps. He ponders over her death, *how did the cobra come to her bedroom?*

As Saleij turns off his smartphone, an old picture gets visible on his inner screen: Thanma chit-chats with her old husband in the love-light, when her baby lies in the valley beneath her breast.

Saleij gets up from the threshold, puts on a white cap and ambles through the parching sunlight, whispering, "Life and weather are alike, always changing beyond imagination."

Money Time

"Welcome to Money Time! Today, we have a special contestant, Kalhani from Idukki, the land of natural charms." The anchorwoman Ervani Allu is slim like a reed, with a vibrant voice.

A close-up of Kalhani's face, like a hyacinth flower above the surface of the muddy water, is visible on the TV screen.

A small house with a red-tiled roof appears in the background. Kalhani stands in the yard with her eyes cast on the nearby tea hill slopes.

The quizmaster Krithik sits in a high-back chair. He is an eminent scholar and orator. He invites Kalhani, the contestant, into the seat in front of him. The setting and the ambient orange glow are enticing.

Kalhani is palpitating. Talcum powder cannot conceal her nerves.

"Cool, Kalhani! Here comes your first question: Who was the first president of India? Was it A: Indira Gandhi, B: Jawaharlal Nehru, C: Dr Rajendra Prasad, or D: Zakir Husain."

Simultaneously the question and multiple-choice options appear on the background of the screen.

"Option C. Dr Rajendra Prasad"

"Are you sure, Kalhani?" Ervani tries to confirm the answer.

"Yes, I'm pretty sure."

"Congratulations! You win 5000 rupees," Krithik applauds.

"Before the second question, let's see Kalhani's family." Ervani turns towards the screen in the background.

A middle-aged woman sits in an old fiber chair in the living room. She is wearing a faded maroon sari and trinkets. Her countenance is like a deadpan mushroom.

Being Human

"Yes, that's my ma, my sole blood relation on the earth. She is a laborer on a tea plantation."

"Well, let me ask you the second question. Who's the author of the book *The Good Earth*?"

Again, the question and options appear on the screen in the background.

"My answer is Pearl S. Buck."

"Right answer, congratulations!"

Kalhani's prize money multiplies. She is all smiles. Ervani claps, taps Kalhani on the shoulder.

"Now, it's time for a short break. We'll come back soon. Stay tuned!"

A charming woman is taking a bath in a lake. Sunshine falls on her half-naked wet body through the gaps in the canopy of leaves. She soaps her shoulders and neck with a yellowish green Layola soap. TV channels earn a lot from commercial advertisements.

"Welcome back!" Ervani addresses viewers with verve.

Before the third question, she asks Kalhani, "How will you spend the prize money?"

Kalhani wants to put up a house. Currently, she stays in a rented house. She got a small plot of land from the Panchayat under the Dream Home Project.

"Well, Kalhani, we hope you can fulfil your dream!"

Ervani's enthralling presentation attracts more viewers. Money Time goes up in the ratings. Peacock Feather is already a popular TV channel.

"Let's go to the next question. Are you ready?"

Kalhani's prize money increases to 30000 rupees, answering the third question. She is riding high. Her heart throbs with joy.

"There was a tragic happening in your life. Am I right?" Ervani asks, having already studied Kalhani's life. To captivate viewers by creating sensation, is a business trick TV channels use in the competitive world.

"Yeah, you're right, Ervani. I'd been living with my mother in a second-hand car dealer's outbuilding. A rented prison. I won several prizes in the literary competitions. Unfortunately, I had neither a shelf nor a coffer to keep my certificates and the other precious belongings. I treasured everything in a cardboard box kept in a nook of the outbuilding.

One day, I went to take part in the literary competition, conducted by Green Ink Association, Thrissur. And it was very late when we returned home.

Our owner had cleaned the outbuilding during our absence. Oh! The cardboard box with my certificates and belongings in it was thrown into the bonfire. Only the ash remained under the coconut palm in the yard."

A rhinoceros can never distinguish between a certificate and waste paper.

"Gosh, how did you react?" Ervani's face fades.

"I wished I could end myself on the spot. I lost everything which had illuminated me in my misery. Those things couldn't be bought with money. Whether he burnt the cardboard box deliberately, or by a mistake, is still unknown."

"I heard that you were hospitalized."

"My veins were frozen. My body was partly paralyzed. It took nearly a month to recover."

Krithik is all ears. Ervani's wet eyes glisten.

"Forget it, Kalhani! To feed on a painful past is to weaken your mind and body. Now you're in the limelight. We all pray for you."

"Thank you, Ervani!"

The fourth question is as hard as a breccia. Yet she's not willing to succumb. After pondering for a couple of minutes, she gives the right answer.

Being Human

"It's time to wind up today's episode. We'll meet at 7:30 P.M. tomorrow. Good night!" Ervani hugs Kalhani, waves to her viewers.

It's Saturday evening. Friday elapsed as a yellow mango leaf fell down.

It's time for the final episode with Kalhani. Ervani wears a white frock with violet and crimson flowers. She creates a spring on the TV.

"Our Kalhani is a good folk singer. She'll sing for us."

Kalhani's voice has a natural charm. Her folk song is about the tea garden workers. The miseries of women who pluck tea leaves echo through the song.

Krithik shoots the fifth question worth 50000 rupees. It's about the largest desert in the world. Kalhani's life itself is a desert with dates of dreams. She picks the right option as if she were a crane catching fish.

"Congratulations! Answering this question, your prize money rises to 50000. How do you feel, Kalhani?"

"I'm very much excited, sir! This amount is far beyond my expectation."

Now images of four white ducks can be seen on the screen in the background.

"Kalhani, please turn to look at the ducks. Examine them minutely, and then find the odd one out within ten seconds," Karthik gives her a task this time.

Kalhani has a keen intellect, chooses the third duck. Unlike the rest, the third one has a tiny dark spot on its neck.

Kalhani has answered for 80000 rupees.

"A young guy wanted to marry you. Am I right?" Ervani is nosy for her viewers.

Her visage speckled with shyness, Kalhani voices her nuptial sorrows. "A real estate agent's son was willing to marry me. My ma too liked the proposal. Being unemployed, he wanted to find a job before the marriage. He told my ma that he was going abroad in search of a job, asked her if she could give him some money as the dowry in advance. My poor ma gave him all her savings."

"When will he return to marry you?"

"He's not likely to come back. Four years have passed since he flew to Mauritius. He never contacted me. There's a rumor that he has married a French lady."

All are silent. Silence is an electrode through which inexpressible emotions pass.

Kalhani is noble, not by birth, but by her own virtue.

"Come back to the game, Kalhani! If you answer the next question, you'll get one-and-a-half lakh rupees. Are you ready now?"

"Yes, sir."

"Who scored the first goal in the 2018 FIFA World Cup?"

It's a difficult question. Kalhani fumbles in her memory. Her eyes bulge.

"Sorry, sir, I quit."

"Well, well, Kalhani! You've won 80000 rupees. Congratulations!"

"Thank you, sir! Being always in poverty, this is a dream-sum."

Kalhani receives the prize money from Krithik. Ecstatic moments unblock her blood vessels clogged with distress.

Ervani asks Kalhani, hugging her, "Finally, what do you tell our viewers?"

"Time redraws life designs."

Kunjan and Kayami

From the land of hills and valleys, Kunjan comes to the west coast of God's Own Country. He and his spouse are in search of a shelter. They are homeless peripatetic laborers.

After a tedious wandering, the couple reaches Umeera's house in the gloaming. Umeera cannot unwelcome them.

She has been alone in her big house for several months. Her one and only daughter has been married off. She lives in the city. It's only when she comes with her naughty boys for holidaying that Umeera's house wakes up from silence.

"You can use my outbuilding, just behind my bedroom." Umeera opens a shelter for Kunjan and Kayami.

Umeera's husband was bedridden for a few years. His muscles were malfunctioning. Sockets below his silvered eyebrows were graves of vision. But he had a sound mind.

"Umii, where're you?" he called out frequently from his bed. His voice created confidence in Umeera, driving her fears away. Unfortunately, that vibrant voice ceased a year ago.

Kunjan smokes beedi and walks to the outbuilding, followed by Kayami, who has put on a faded tawny sari. He slings a white cloth bag, which is dusty, and with brown stains, over his shoulder. There is an old aluminum box in Kayami's hand.

Thunder rumbles. Nowadays the weather is truly eccentric.

These coolies will save me from loneliness, Umeera muses. After her husband's demise, Umeera has been experiencing a variety of fears within the walls of loneliness.

Last night, Umeera slept long like a brown bat.

9 A.M.

Being Human

Dawn chill still lingers in the morning air. She brushes her teeth, washes her face with cool water. Then she comes out to the portico. Kunjan and Kayami have already been installed in the yard, exposed to the soft sunshine. Umeera whispers, staring at them through her red-rimmed spectacles, "Good *kani!*" Kani is a vernacular word meaning the first sight of the day. *Whether a day will be good or bad depends on kani,* Umeera too believes like others.

"Didn't you sleep well?" Umeera initiates a chit-chat.

"We did, though mosquitoes drained our blood." Kayami says, rubbing her brown cheek.

Slowly Umeera delves into their life, their secrets and misfortunes intrigue her. She is a typical countrywoman with a craving for calumnies.

She puts forward certain terms in no uncertain terms. Kunjan and Kayami can stay in her outbuilding free of rent, provided that they sweep her floor every day, wash her clothes, and help her dry coconut kernels. They accept Umeera's conditions with alacrity.

There are many expatriates' houses in this coastal village. The expats struggle to earn in the Arabian Desert, while their wives live in luxury. Though it's hard to tame their prancing passion, most of them keep chastity.

Laborers are always in demand here. Yet the local working class people repeat, "We've no job." Basically, they are unwilling to work. What they like most is to sit simply in laziness like a crow-pheasant.

Kunjan and Kayami do housework here and there every day. They live silently, sleep soundly. Among the tiny twigs of life, they twitter like sunbirds, free from maelstroms.

How quickly one month passes! They get accustomed to the ways of the new village. Kayami assists Umeera in the kitchen every evening.

Compared to other days, Sundays pass fast. Today is a bleary Sunday. People have already been informed about the solar eclipse. They should not stare at the sun directly with bare eyes. The sun is expected to come out in splendor by noon. Suddenly Kunjan feels chest pain that radiates to his left arm and shoulder. "Kayami…KAYAMI…," his voice rises in ache. Soon he swoons in sweat.

Next week, Kunjan undergoes a coronary bypass surgery. It takes four hours to complete the surgery successfully.

How to meet the hospital expenses? The question grows gigantic in Kayami's mind.

She borrows a huge amount from Umeera.

After nine days, Kunjan is brought back to the outbuilding. The cardiologist has advised him to take rest. He must avoid climbing the stairs and onerous works. Kayami takes care of him well under the parasol of love. They are left to sink or swim.

It takes just a fortnight for Umeera's compassion to run out. She demands Kayami her money back.

Kayami journeys through the dawn light to her distant home village of hills and valleys, where she owns three cents of land, her sole property. She has to repay Umeera the debt. Debt is a smoldering thing in mind. She has made up her mind to sell her land.

Kunjan burns in boredom in the outbuilding. He discerns the depth of Kayami's absence. Love grows in the longing to see the beloved.

The day blooms bright. Umeera spreads coconut kernels on the jute sacks laid in the yard. It will take two days minimum to get the coconut kernels dried in the parching sunlight. Coconut oil is extracted from the dried kernel called copra.

Quite unexpectedly, weather turns cloudy. Umeera fears that the kernels will be steeped in rain. She needs the assistance of somebody to take the kernels upstairs storeroom. Forgetting Kunjan's cardiac condition, she seeks his help.

Kunjan is never sassy, doesn't know how to say, 'No.' Dependence is a curse. A mouse-cursor relationship is patent between Umeera and Kunjan.

Being Human

He longs for Kayami's presence. Through the drizzle, he collects coconut kernels in a sack and carries it to the upstairs storeroom. Then he climbs down the stairs and darts to the yard swiftly to take the next sack of kernels, puffing and panting.

"Kunjan, come on…FAST," Umeera spurs him.

Kunjan finishes his work in sweat. Unloading the fifth sack of kernels, he climbs down, swaying in fatigue. Like a dummy, he falls down.

Hearing the thud, Umeera comes to the staircase. She stands dumbfounded before Kunjan's still body. Shrieking, shouting…she calls her neighbors.

The number you're trying to call is currently switched off. A voice message from Vodafone. Again, Umeera tries to call Kayami, but in vain.

Following the Covid-19 protocol, Kunjan's body is cremated in the Public Crematorium. Only two neighbors and three health department officials attended the funeral.

"Kayami…" Umeera wakes up from the midday nap, looking around. She has neither read nor heard of an auditory hallucination. *A vibrant voice from beyond death!* She wonders and believes it.

Where did Kayami go? Will she ever come back? Umeera prays for Kayami not to return. She yearns to nap again, but she can't, for something pricks her.

Mosquito Coil

A parching wind unveils her head. Feeling exposed, she covers her black coconut oiled hair again with her beige silk shawl. She walks along the long sand path leading to my house. Her footfall on the tiny pebbles in my yard. I return from Kabul in *And the Mountains Echoed* by Khaled Hosseini, and raise my eyes. Her chubby cheeks are red, maybe due to shyness or sizzling summer sunshine. She stands wearily before my threshold. Soon her son, who was trudging behind her in the eccentric weather, nears her and hides among the faded blooms in her maxi.

Hers is a face familiar to me. She had come to borrow money from my spouse twice or thrice previously. She doesn't move her tongue. She won't, I know. Being noble to her core, she is reluctant to beg even in her penury. But now she must do it, at least secretly. Tugging at her maxi, her four-year-old son points his index finger towards the banana fritter on the Chinese plate on the nearby *thinna* on the veranda. The woman gives a soft tap on his head.

I ask her to ring the doorbell. The front door is often kept closed to create a divine world of loneliness on the veranda. From my hanging cane chair, I can enjoy the bright flowers and butterflies, or listen to the twitter, not electronic, of tiny birds from the hibiscus twigs. Lots of sweet emotions die unheard in their voice.

Hearing the bell, my wife opens the front door. The spicy smell of fish frying in hot coconut oil also comes out.

"Thaatha...[3]" This is a word of respect and politeness used to address a woman here. "Could you please lend me a thousand rupees?" With a pale smile capping all her miseries, she begs in a low voice. My wife goes in without uttering anything, and then comes back with a two hundred rupee note. My spouse knows well that this unfortunate woman is behindhand. Receiving the paltry sum, the discontented lady turns to go.

---

[3] *An elderly sister.*

Being Human

"Hey, child…," I raise my voice, when the poor lady and her son return with the beggarly sum.

Both of them turn back. I hold out the banana fritter towards the boy. He gazes at his mother, and then slowly comes to take it from my hand.

"Why do you need a thousand rupees, Roshma? I forgot to ask you," my wife cannot control her curiosity.

"Didn't you hear about yesterday's tragic incident?" Mrs. Radheen begins with a question.

Yesterday.

The mosque at Manathala had been decorated flamboyantly. Around twenty caparisoned elephants stood in a row in front of the mosque. Music of the modern rock band and the traditional *chenda* vibrates the crowd in the gloaming. Thousands of people, irrespective of religion, gathered in and around the mosque. Radheen had been installed close to the elephants moving their ears rhythmically. Really that was a regional festival, more than a religious one, conducted in remembrance of the martyrdom of the valiant warrior Hydrosekutty Moopppar, who fought for truth and justice, and who got eternal rest in the courtyard of the mosque.

Unfortunately, one of the elephants was perturbed. It trumpeted and turned its head back. Radheen was undaunted, did not move a bit, blinded by the festive delight. The fireworks turned that elephant jittery. Those elephants once lived in the serenity of the woods. Who remembered such truth? Quite unexpectedly, that disturbed elephant caught Radheen with its long trunk and hurled him in the air. He fell down with a thud. Timely intervention of the mahouts saved his life.

"Where's Radheen now?"

"He's been brought back from hospital. His right leg is broken. Spinal injuries too. His body is a bundle of pain. He's to lie on his back, taking rest for a long time," Roshma's words really upset me. Her neighbors are not likely to help her much because Roshma and Radheen are not indigenous.

They stay in a rented room, doing casual work. Their native village is in Palakkad district.

As the mother and son walk back along the torrid way, an old love story unfolds in my mind. Yes, my spouse had told me:

The smell of new clothes and romance lingered in Toyano Fashion World, where the cat eyed Radheen was a salesman, and Roshma a saleswoman. Their love burgeoned beyond the usual chit-chat.

As a result of the unexpected *hartal* in the afternoon following the murder of a local political leader, things went haywire in Palakkad district. An amalgam of sounds – of shops shutting down, protest slogans, siren wailing and so on – could be heard. Radheen and Roshma had resolved not to go home. People were hurrying home in panic. Radheen biked through the gaps in the mob. Roshma's arms entwined him like a vine. Nobody could recognize her in burqa.

They arrived at the foot of Cheppara, which is a gigantic rock, as large as a mountain.

Radhenn locked his bike under a coconut palm. Then they began to climb the rock hand in hand. Night concealed the natural charms. All the other visitors had left the place. On reaching the deserted top, they looked around. Being fatigued, they sat on the barren rock. She removed her burqa and wiped sweat drops from her forehead and nape with a soft kerchief. His cotton vest had steeped in sweat. After some time, she took out the food parcel, opening her vanity bag. The spicy smell of the curry wafted up from the parcel. Fuelled by hunger, they ate their supper – *parotta*[4] and beef curry – voraciously.

Stepping down, they wandered among the trees and partly dried shrubs. Moonlight slipped down through the gaps in the canopy of leaves. They watched a dark cobra creeping among the fallen leaves under a wild plant,

---

[4] *Flat bread.*

which was full of red blooms. They felt it crawling through their veins. And her soft fleshy arms entwined his burly body.

Still it was not dawn. Misty. Roshma put on her burqa, shivering. She woke her lover up, who was snoring on the bare sand. Both of them huddled together and waited for the sun.

It spread like a forest fire that Roshma eloped with Radheen. He had no relative other than a wizened aunt. Roshma was also almost in the same condition. She had a rheumatic mother to take care of. Her hunchback father, a vacuous man, lived with another woman, a street dancer, in Tamil Nadu.

There was a frenzied crowd in front of Toyano Fashion World. Radheen was a Muslim, and Roshma a Hindu. That communal factor exacerbated the situation. No one considered them as human beings with blood and passion. The people forgot that God was the invisible universal power permeating all living and non-living things.

Soon Radheen received a phone call from one of his friends. He perceived the peril in store for them in their native village. So they sought shelter in the house of one of their colleagues. After a week, that colleague and his father helped Radheen and Roshma register and legalize their marriage. They were thrown out from home, Toyano Fashion World and many minds.

"I'll visit Radheen soon," I assure Roshma, who turns to go, holding her son's dusty wrist

After racking my brain, I have taken a divine decision. In the evening, I knock on the door of their rented room. My wife observes things around silently. Radheen's woeful voice chanting holy verses leaks out through the cracks in the wooden door,

Roshma, who is lachrymose, opens the door. Her son welcomes us with an innocent smile. Entering in, we sit beside Radheen. He stops chanting and looks at me. Anxieties about his spouse and son – more than about himself – echo through his voice and expression. He cannot do any work for an indefinite period. I see misery face to face in its concrete form. There is no trace of romance. Only food and medicine dominate their thoughts.

Both the comforter and the comforted get relief and pleasure from a true soothing. It's time for us to say goodbye. We get up. My wife whispers in Roshma's ears. We walked to our car with Roshma following closely behind. We have kept rice, grocery and so on in the trunk, which will help Roshma's family keep their heads above water. Everything is brought in. Radheen is silent. We seem to grow in his moist eyes.

After a fortnight.

I'm wide-eyed at the sight of Roshma, who comes with a cloth bag of mosquito coils. As an eye adjusting itself to darkness, she adapts to her desert-life. A camel-like adaptation.

"How is Radheen?"

"By *Padachon's*[5] grace, his condition is improving."

"You started a new business?"

Her smile with a shade of shyness adds charm to her countenance.

"I sell mosquito coils for a company at Thrissur. I get a paltry sum as commission, barely enough to buy bread and medicine."

I bought a pack of mosquito coils.

The mosquito coil smolders on my veranda. Again, I create the creative loneliness, shutting the front door. Evil mosquitoes fall down; sublime thoughts flutter in the fragrant smoke.

---

[5] *A vernacular word meaning God.*

Mysterious Peringadam

I mistrust that Kayyoma's father was killed by a holy tree, though she and several others disagree with me.

An old three-storied building with a tiled roof is the one and only house on my grandma's land, which is locally known as Peringadam. After my grandma's death, owls, temple doves, crickets, Norway rats and mongooses are the dwellers in this mansion.

Peringadam is two acres of land without a compound wall. Kayyoma, with a deadpan visage, totters across Peringadam, which is full of wild plants and trees. Even at her seventy, she finds herself her livelihood as a sweeper.

Kayyoma's hut stands close to the boundary of Peringadom. It's no longer a coconut grove. Gliricidia trees and Communist Pacha shrubs thrive everywhere on the land. Wild creepers asphyxiate each positive growth.

As her fellow countrymen, Kayyoma too, dreads to tread the path across Peringadam at night.

This land has always been a grove of mysteries. Even a stray cat's eye turns spooky. Many people residing around are ignorant and superstitious, with minds conducive for rich growth of ghostly things.

I

Kayyoma's father was enjoying the full moon. The red roof of Peringadam house and the portia tree blooms in the front yard, with a rare charm in the moonlight, enthralled him.

Soon he noticed one of his hens wandering out of the coop. As he pursued, it flew and perched on the lowest branch of the cashew tree at the edge of Peringadam. Then it began to cluck. He looked up, pondering how to catch it.

Being Human

He couldn't make out what was happening. Petrified, he looked again. It was soil falling down through the gaps in the canopy of cashew leaves. He looked up and around, finding nobody. He dashed back home, without stopping.

I

"Where're you going, Baby?" Kayyoma inquires in a soft voice.

"To sit on the old steps."

"Be careful, dear! Peringadam is not a safe place," she utters not many words, but she means much.

I'm escaping from the hot confinement within my concrete house. Disdaining her words, I stroll on. Peringadam is a haunted place, not for me, but for the inhabitants around. The land is thick green with a photogenic face. At night, the place is scarier with the reality of reptiles and fantasy of spooky creatures.

My God! Never seen it before! A long fat snake in charming blue creeps fast in front. It's as strange as the superstitions existing in and around Peringadam. With all my eyes, I watch it zigzag into the depth of thick Communist Pacha shrubs, imprinting an eternal eerie image on my mind.

Though Peringadam house disappeared in the time-bin, its steps remain as my family's past glory. It's nostalgic to sit on the old steps that led to a sand path across a paddy field. Walking along this path, one can reach the tarred highway.

I am all ears, listening to the sunbirds among the henna twigs. Each sound in nature has a meaning, often incomprehensible to the human world.

While cogitating about mysteries around, Kayyoma's father dies again in my mind.

I

It happened in 1956, the same year Kerala State was formed, when Kayyoma was six years old. Her father returned home from Peringadam, after cutting a wild tree, the name of which was unknown to him. Within a couple of hours, his body began to swell, frightening him. He was reticent, kept everything hidden from his spouse.

After an early supper, boiled cassava with sardine curry, he went to sleep on his mat.

Fresh sun-blooms fell down through the chinks in his coconut leaf roof. He couldn't sleep well, itching. He took his frameless broken mirror, waking up from his mat. His swollen clumsy face fills his mind with forebodings. He looked like a python.

Before noon, there was a crowd in Kayyoma's yard. It was really a bolt from the blue. How did it happen? The wood-cutter was a robust man with brawny arms.

"Certainly, he was killed by a holy tree. The curse of a dying tree is deadly." Kochu, the Ancient Man of the village, who was a superstition-making machine, opined.

|

Enticed by the fragrance, I get up from the old steps and pluck a bunch of henna flowers. An olfactory thrill. Like the smell of the heart of the earth.

O which is that bird darting into the large pond? I have seen white-breasted water-hens on the verge of the Peringadam Pond, where vetiver grass thrives.

Now what Kochu's son, with goosebumps, told me once floats down my memory lane.

|

The pond was the main source of drinking water in the area. Women collected pure water, as pellucid as teardrops, in pots and buckets.

Being Human

One dawn, Kochu's mother was collecting water from the pond. It was misty. Frighteningly, she heard the clinking of chains. She stood straight, looked around. Nothing. *Was it real?*

She stooped again to fill her pots. The same sound recurred. She wanted to shriek, but no sound came out. Her vocal cords were frozen. It took a few minutes to move her legs. She returned home with empty pots, panting.

Later, she knew that her friend too had the same experience.

People believed in the invisible presence of a Chain Man in the pond.

Dates? Very enticing! It's incredible to see this wild tree bear fruits. *Fruit or nut?* It's like a date in shape. The tree stands close to the old steps, my favorite hang-out. I have never thought about its name. My unruly curiosity prances; I pluck a bunch of *Peringadam dates*, bending the lowest branch.

How astonished she will be! My wife is very fond of dates. So I hurry home with the strange *dates,* dark green in hue.

"Peringadam dates... Peringadam dates..."

My spouse comes out. She's surprised to find Peringadam dates in my hand. She takes one and looks at it. *Not dates.* Finding it hard, she picks up a stone to crack the pod. *It's a wild nut.* She flings the nut away in dismay. Unfortunately, she's not aware of its white sap spread over her arms.

A devotional song from the nearby temple floats in the air. Devotees call it *5 P.M. Song.*

My arms itch. I scratch. Itch...scratch...itch...scratch... Red rashes appear on my skin.

"See this..." My wife's voice wavers. Her face and arms have swelled appallingly.

Next day. A morning breeze blows through the golden sunshine. I cannot enjoy natural charms with a perturbed mind. Sitting in my recliner, I scratch on – itch touches the roof of my brain. My wife's condition is worse. Her entire body has swelled alarmingly with red rashes. Tablets and ointment, prescribed by our physician the previous night, utterly fail before itching.

"You had better consult with Vishatti." Kayyoma drops valuable advice, realizing my itchy plight. Yes, an illiterate woman illuminates a learned man.

Vishatti is a widow, who dwells in another village, east of Peringadam. She stares at my wife, with her left arm buttressing her head. She has an antique face. Her protruding veins are like roots of a banyan tree. More than a doctor, she is an expert, with the traditional knowledge and practical wisdom, in treating snake bites. People say that her body is poison-proof – even a Malabar pit viper's venom won't work in her veins.

Watching carefully the image of the tree and its dark green nuts on my Smartphone, Vishatti declares, "No doubt, it's Cheru, a very toxic tree!" She examines my wife's arm. "Cheru is highly allergic, may even cause death. As a remedy, people undressed and hugged a Thanni tree in ancient times. There was, and is, no other medicine."

Thanni is its vernacular name; and Terminalia Billerica scientific name. *Where could we find the tree?* My wife and I look at each other.

"Don't worry about hugging the tree, naked. You had better go to an Ayurvedic medical shop, where you get a bark of Thanni. You grind the bark and apply it on your skin."

"OK, thank you! I would like to know your consultation fee?"

"No, I don't charge any fee. When you're cured, don't forget to visit me with some jackfruit leaves for my goats."

Vishatti's medicine works wonders. Swelling and itching disappear slowly.

A toxic tree and an anti-toxic tree; sin and redemption! Nature is amazing. Google tells me medicinal values of both trees.

Being Human

"Kayyoma Thatha… I found it … I found it" My cry of joy stops Kayyoma on her way. She is returning from some house after her work.

"What do you mean, Baby?"

"You see that tree?" I raise my index finger.

"Yeah!"

"That's Cheru. Highly allergic and toxic! It may even turn fatal in some bodies."

"Who told?" Her eyes open wide.

"Vishatti told me so. Thanks for your advice to consult with her!"

"Welcome, Baby! Glad that you went to Vishatti!"

"Now you can imagine how your father died."

"How?'

"The tree, which your father had cut, was a Cheru. Quite possible, its toxic sap penetrated his skin, affecting him mortally."

"No, he was killed by a holy tree." With a frown, she walks to her house.

There is no holy tree on Peringadam. But Kayyaoma can never alter her belief.

Foolish beliefs and fancies of the locals are more beautiful than scientific truths.

What make Peringadam charming are nature as well as mysteries in and around.

God-man

A bearded holy man in saffron dhoti chants wedding mantras. Pranoy has been installed like a puppet on the dais. An artificial smile hides his shyness. His bride has put on a cream sari with a matching blouse. A thick blush spreads on her face. The ritualistic ululation and drum beats begin. Quite unexpectedly, she takes off the wedding garland of jasmine blooms from her neck, tears it to pieces, and then gets down from the dais. Everybody is flummoxed.

"O God! What happened to you, Rupa?"

"I'm sorry, Ma. I don't want this marriage."

"Are you insulting us, idiot?" Rupa's uncle loses his temper.

"Forgive me, uncle. I can't marry him," Rupa's voice shivers. She goes to her bedroom and locks its door from inside.

Pranoy's plastic smile vanishes. He regrets his ill-mannered gestures and expressions on the dais, created by his diffidence. A dark shade covers his countenance. Guests leave Rupa's house, pouring buckets of coarse words on her. Her mother with a heavy head sits on the floor, leaning against a grey pillar in front of the house. She longs for her husband's presence, the solace of his words, though in vain. Rupa's uncle, lost in gloom, paces up and down in the yard, smoking a beedi.

Pain fades, exposed to time. Pranoy has been transferred. He comes to the office of the new school with the transfer order. Signing the attendance, he asks a strange funny question to the headmaster.

"Sir, can I go home now?"

"No, you can't. Our school time is from 10 A.M. to 3.30 P.M."

The headmaster, who is an austere person, senses something strange in the new teacher's behavior. He mutters as Pranoy leaves the room, "This man will certainly be a hairy caterpillar, causing itch always."

Being Human

Though intelligent, Pranoy often behaves as a crackpot. This may be his trick to escape teaching. He loiters in an empty nook at break, never goes to the staffroom.

Rain starts again after a fortnight. The school yard looks like a garden of umbrellas in various hues. Some students and teachers are partly wet, for their raincoats and umbrellas cannot resist heavy showers. Pranoy, bundled up in a black raincoat, pushes open the school gate. Without removing the raincoat, he enters in, wetting the office floor. Taking a blue biro from his shirt's pocket, he signs in the attendance register kept on the headmaster's table.

"Why are you late?" the headmaster stares at his watch.

"Heavy rain, sir."

Pranoy musters his courage to ask an odd question.

"Since I came late, can I go home early, sir?"

Seeing the headmaster's eyes bulging behind the thick glasses of his spectacles, Pranoy scoots from the office.

On the way to the class, he comes across the music teacher, a lanky brown lady. He talks to her as if to an old acquaintance.

"I don't like to teach the school children."

His words startle her.

"My ambition was to become a college lecturer."

"Did you try for that?''

"Yeah. I did. I approached the manager of Gurukulam College at Kothanadu, but who advised me to take an M.Phil degree, in addition to my M A in English literature."

"Sir, I think M.Phil degree is a desirable qualification."

"Yeah. After taking M.Phil from the University of Calicut, I went to meet the manager again. He greeted me warmly, offered me a chair in his office. He ordered milk tea for me. Then he explained slowly the change in policy to appoint a lecturer in his college. I must do research in literature, hold a Ph.D."

"Alas! You dropped your dream, didn't you?"

"No, ma'am, I decided to do research."

"Good!" the music teacher appreciates him.

"I approached the manager once again. He congratulated me on my academic excellence, while going through the certificates. Soon his face faded. He told me politely that I crossed the prescribed age limit for appointment."

Pity begins to grow in her mind.

Pranoy's life has been a mash-up of learning and laziness. The funniest thing about him is that he enjoys his own idiocy. He is certainly a man with vast learning, yet sometimes he behaves oddly. He often asks his colleagues, "Do you think I am a misfit?"

Last bell rings. He flees to his rented room, two hundred feet away from his school. On entering his abode, he flings his bag to a corner, takes his official dress off, and then puts a lungi and a T-shirt on. Lighting his kerosene stove with a matchstick, he parches rice and pounds it in a small granite mortar. He puts the rice powder into a big cup of steaming black tea, adds some jaggery powder, and stirs it with a steel spoon, making a brown cream. Now that a familiar crow peers at the cup from a fence of thatched coconut leaves, he takes a teaspoonful of the rice cream and throws it out. The crow lands on the yard to peck at the thick cream. This black bird is his one and only visitor.

Left alone, memories haunt him from a decade-old past. Fragments of Rupa's figure still remain in his soul. Why did she refuse to marry him on the wedding day? No doubt, her lover, a notorious sorcerer of the village, applied some sorcery. Pranoy firmly believes that the sole valid reason for his mental turbulence is the black magic that Rupa's lover applies.

Gradually, Pranoy gets accustomed to the ways of the new school. He is captivated by the charm of a physics teacher, wife of an immigrant. As she always wears sari that her husband sends from Muscat, she is called 'foreign sari' among her colleagues. Pranoy's introverted traits disappear before her presence, he becomes eloquent. It seems that the repressed love is emerging from him.

Pranoy returns to his abode earlier than usual. He has decided to celebrate his 45th birthday, cutting the cake he bought from a bakery in the town. He throws out a piece of the cake to the crow. It crows as if wishing him a happy birthday and lands on the ground to feed on the piece of cake. Nobody knows that he is the first man who celebrates his birthday with a crow.

Pranoy's laziness grows with the day. He behaves like an insane man, creates a kind of baffling situation in the classroom. He begins to sing a song that can in no way be connected with the topic he teaches. Some naughty boys encourage him, clapping. After a wild dance, he even ventures to perform a circus and falls down with a thud. Has he consumed alcohol or smoked a cannabis beedi? Obviously the thought-producing machine in his brain malfunctions. A studious girl records complete pandemonium stealthily, using her mobile phone camera. The last period on Friday ends thus with the long bell.

The girl's video clip goes viral.

"Dismiss him from the school!"

Parents raise a storm of protest. They can't put up with Pranoy's anarchic behavior in the classroom, which is likely to ruin the reputation of the school. The headmaster telephones the Deputy Director of Education.

Pranoy is suspended from the service. He makes up his mind to move away. The crow perches on the fence, as usual. He comes out with a large leather bag, holding it with both hands, and dawdles to the tarred road. Sweat drops appear on his forehead. The crow flutters its wings and flies way.

One more day drowns in darkness. Pranoy alights from the bus at Mavu and walks to his parents' house. As he opens the gate with a clang, his dad, a shriveled old man, gets up from the arm chair nap on the veranda. He is alone at home after his wife's death a couple of months ago. A maid regularly comes in the morning to cook food and wash clothes for him. He is tickled pink by his son's unexpected arrival. Pranoy drops his bag down and hugs his dad, hiding his secret sorrows.

He is compelled to share his dad's porridge for supper. After a quarter-hour, the smell of burning paper spreads in the air from the kitchen. Flames chew Pranoy's certificates. He is in utter dismay.

"What's the smell, Pranoy?"

"Don't worry, dad. That's waste paper burning."

Pranoy's dad feels a slight pain in his chest and soon falls asleep in the arm chair, exposed to the night wind that gives transient relief from the summer heat.

Hearing the usual devotional song from a nearby temple, he wakes up, rubbing his eyes. Morning is not morning yet.

"Where're you to, my son?"

"To see a friend. I'll return soon, dad."

Pranoy hastens through the dew drops. Admittedly, too much learning has turned him lazy and eccentric. He is chagrined; he reaches in a woody valley before the noon.

He wants to lead a life free from the frets like a carefree forest man in the past. Wandering in the forest, he enjoys each line from nature's anthology. Suddenly, he is petrified at the sight of an orange striped snake creeping among the dried leaves in front. He changes his path, increasing pace. His legs are beginning to tire. Seeing a human shape emerge from the green thicket at his right side, he stops. The stranger comes near to question him, pointing a gun.

Being Human

The stranger is impressed with Pranoy's polite ways. He takes Pranoy to the deep wood, offering him food and shelter. They enter a temporary shed, put up with blue tarpaulin. A tall lady, wearing a silver nose ring, cooks sweet potatoes in an aluminum vessel. She has kept a gun near the bamboo pole that buttresses the roof of the tent.

What happened to my son? Pranoy's dad is perturbed. Now he seems to see his son's head with black hair, close to the gate. He looks, rubbing his eyes. But that is a crow preening itself, perched on the gate. He reclines on the chair again, expecting that his son will come back soon.

One month passes by leaps and bounds. Revolutionaries in the forest are silent most of the time. Being fed up with their teachings, Pranoy has made up his mind to escape from the confinement. They discuss attacking a government office. Pranoy doesn't like weapon and violence. He cannot sleep; he twists and turns in a coir mat, while the revolutionaries are fast asleep. Getting up, he flees through the midnight forest. Even the rustling of leaves produces waves of fear.

It is dawn. Pranoy falls down under a peepal tree on the side of a dirt road. There is nothing in his pocket. His empty stomach begins to burn. Blindly he stretches his hand before a lady with the skin color of black tea. Bristles have developed as a black beard on his chin and cheeks, giving him a God-man's look. His face that is august with lustrous eyes enchants her. She stands before him with her hands folded and then puts a ten-rupee coin on his palm. Pranoy is delighted. He says softly, lifting his right hand, "God bless you!" She smiles and strolls along the dirt road. Fortunately he has reached in one of the most superstitious villages in the country. The shade of peepal tree is his new shelter.

Next morning, another woman comes, saying, "Baba, bless me too!" She puts a cloth bag containing rice, an ash-guard, a pumpkin, and a pack of banana chips at Pranoy's feet.

The title, 'Baba' excites him. It is a word of respect and divinity.

"My sister-in-law's son has been trying for a visa to work in Qatar for a couple of months. He got it yesterday by your grace," the strange woman goes on.

A new door opens in the mist of life. News about new Baba spreads like dengue. More people come, seeking his blessings. False belief is also a source of relief. It dawns on Pranoy that the village needs a God-man to fall back on. He can flourish in the shade of peepal tree, exploiting the ignorance of the inhabitants. Books he had read start working in his mind. His face is plastered with thick mystery.

"I killed that idle idiot called Pranoy," the God-man mumbles under his breath. People come in large numbers seeking his grace, and he grows with their grace.

Peeping Palunni

He hides in a thicket on the canal bank with his lecherous eyes cast on the half-naked girls.

Kanoli canal with its girdle of coconut palms glitters in the bright sunshine. It was built during the British rule in India. Most of the inhabitants are poor coolies. The girls float like ducks on the water, while their mothers wash dirty dhotis, shirts, saris, and under-clothes.

Evil thoughts warm Palunni up. Sweat drops appear on his forehead. His hidden spy camera gobbles the half-nude wet girls; its stomach is almost full.

The traditional dress of a Kanoli woman is a sari covering her body from the neck to toes. Even a bit of feminine nudity becomes an epicenter of temptation for Kanoli guys.

Palunni's mother Kallu recalls how the women folk admired her for giving birth to a male child on the eve of Onam, their harvest festival. She had many visitors on that day. They brought baby talc, soap and dress for the newborn baby.

The baby was cute in its layette. Kallu called her baby 'Palunni' meaning 'milk-baby' in her mother tongue.

Now Palunni is a fifteen-year-old student, truly a truant. Lean with sunken eyes. He has grown up, losing the charms of innocence.

Palunni has got a gift, a binocular, from his father Chandru in Dubai. He perambulates on the Kanoli bank, enjoying through his binocular beauty of the local and the migratory Siberian birds.

"Are you blind? Don't you see a woman bathing here?" a maid's unexpected cry startles Palunni, who is wandering on the canal bank with the binocular.

"Sorry, I didn't notice you," he paces back gently. An indecent idea comes into his mind. Soon he scurries into the thicket and hides there behind the net of leaves. Though timid, he enjoys that maid's brown body – magnified through his binocular – in the crystal clear water. This scene creates hot feelings in his mind. He leers at her again and again, his body temperature rises swiftly. Like a blue ecstasy through the binocular.

Kallu is unable to rein her son back. Her son's 'blue-adventure' puts her deep in shame. The binocular takes Palunni to different nooks of nudity. He discontinues his studies, and never attempts for a career.

Sunday twilight, Palunni loiters in the bus station at Chava. He eyes an insurance officer with a cell phone. The light blinks in orange and yellow hues on his phone, while attending a call. Palunni gazes at that mobile set in wonder. As the officer gets on the bus, Palunni follows him. He sits beside him, looking out. The insurance officer keeps his cell phone in the pocket of his white cotton trousers. Now the bus sets off. Soon a snooze begins to swing his head softly.

After half an hour, as his fellow traveler falls asleep, Palunni gently presses on the officer's pocket with his fist. The cell phone slips out of the pocket as a baby out of womb. Palunni takes the phone, and then alights from the bus at the next stop.

He begins his 'hot browsing'. Evil thoughts hide the light of cyber world. He plunges into the bottom of international and interracial nudity. This is an addiction, as hazardous as hashish. Porn sites pervert his vision.

"Palunni's not a little child now. He's grown up, yet there is no change in his character. He always causes troubles," Kallu is down in the mouth.

"I know, I know. But what'll we do in his case?" Chandru asks his wife dolefully, sipping his morning tea. He has returned home from Dubai for the holidays.

"He's twenty-five now. It's better to conduct his marriage."

"I'm also thinking in that way," there is a glare of hope in Chandru's words. "But, who'll give him a girl?"

"Yes, that's the question. He does nothing. Everybody knows his adventures."

Both the parents are really in a quandary.

Ishamu, one of the rich men on the Kanoli bank, has reached home from Bahrain to spend holidays with his spouse. *A reunion after a long interval.* Palunni smells the 'possibility', and approaches Ishamu's house. His arms get scratches while clambering the concrete fence. Through a narrow gap of the bedroom window, he fills his mind and cell phone camera with the hot live scenes.

Midnight steeps in blue moonlight. Palunni returns along an embankment. Suddenly he sees a lady with long black hair walking up and down in the harvested paddy farm. She has put on a white sari. More petrifying is a pair of her protruding white teeth. He darts to his house, mistaking the white figure for a ghost of some peasant woman. The 'ghost' is really a young maniac, an addict to cannabis. He chuckles at Palunni's flight, putting off his wig and artificial teeth.

It's a cloudy morning. Villagers chase Palunni with bamboo sticks, and he runs like a Norway rat. Finding no other way, he dives into the canal. People also leap behind him. A villager seizes Palunni's shirt's collar and drags him onto the sandy bank

"No, I didn't do anything…," Palunni pleads not guilty.

People 'gently handle' his body with the bamboo sticks.

"Sure. He'll never peep into another bathroom," a corpulent middle-aged woman says aloud. "We've given him the right punishment," a peppery old man remarks, dropping his stick.

How quickly the folk disappeared! Palunni's nose has swollen like a cricket ball. Evil blood oozes out from the wounds. He sprawls on the ground motionless.

Chandru and Kallu are sitting in the yard, immersed in thought. They catch sight of a shambling fellow coming towards them. The shaggy figure opens the gate with difficulty.

Being Human

"Palunni!" Chandru stands up embarrassed. Kallu dashes to the gate and embraces his son.

"What happened, Palu?" Kallu asks, crying.

Pulling her arms apart, Palunni walks slowly to his bedroom. Chandru and Kallu follow him closely behind. Palunni slams the door shut, and locks it from inside. His parents knock at the door repeatedly in vain. It remains closed.

Chandru can't sleep. He turns and twists in his bed, while his spouse sobs silently. Night seems too long.

Fresh sun rays warm the frozen emotions up. There is a mug of steaming black tea on the teapoy. Chandru searches in the fragile pages of a telephone directory, which is partly eaten by white ants. He scribbles a phone number on the overleaf of a torn pharmacy bill, and then looks at what he scribbled through his thick glasses. Taking his phone, he dials '0487 5206011', which is the landline number of Mangalya Marriage Bureau at Chava Town.

After three hours.

"She's a perfect match for your son. I inquired about your son on the way. He's very 'famous'. Ha! Ha!" The marriage bureau executive, who is very quick and shrewd in dealing with his clients, takes out a brown squint-eyed girl's photo from his cotton bag and hands it over to Chandru.

"Please, help us somehow," Kallu pleads with the executive.

"She's squint-eyed," Chandru cannot hide his scrupulousness.

"That's not a problem. Her character is good. Nowadays it's difficult to get such a girl," the executive becomes eloquent about the girl, when a loud cracking sound is heard from the kitchen.

Palunni comes out of the kitchen with a visage red with rage, who has overheard everything.

He stares at the executive and cries out, "GET UP, you son of a..."

"Palu, what's this? Cool down. What harm did he do?" Chandru chimes in.

"I don't want marriage. Leave me alone." Palunni snatches at the tea-cup in the executive's hand and flings it to the floor. Everybody startles. The executive slinks to the road.

Kallu and Chandru look at one another with moist eyes.

After a fortnight. Darkness swallows saffron splendor in the western sky. Lured by the light in the bathroom, he approaches gingerly. Oblivion is a boon for him. The rustic lady in the bathroom screams, seeing a pair of lustful eyes. Palunni flees.

Blows and scolding cannot scare him, alter his erotic instinct. He wanders like a rooster in the moonlight, pondering, 'Hiding is a risk, but peeping, a pleasure.'

The Undaunted Swimmer

Wind blows unceasingly, scattering leaves and the fragrance of ylang-ylang flowers in the moonlight. Dropping the cigarette butt, Eanu walks to the waiting room. He installs himself in a chair beside a tubby woman, who is whispering a mysterious mantra.

After a few minutes, a nurse comes out of the delivery room, looking for Eanu.

"It's over. The mother and the baby are fine. Please buy this medicine."

The nurse hands over a prescription to Eanu, who hurries out. A rare emotion sparkles in his eyes.

Now that it's a cesarean delivery, Eanu has to pay a huge amount towards the hospital expenses.

Soon his rapture slips into the abyss of anxiety. *Will my son walk like other children? How can he escape when a stray dog comes to attack him?*

With a growing apprehension, Eanu returns to Qatar, where he is an employee in an oil company. He has already employed a maid to assist his spouse Kayyu.

Baby Shahzil sleeps in the crib. Kayyu watches her son's ethereal smile in sleep. Often her pleasures end in pangs. Her friends and relatives express concern over the infant. Kayyu keeps silent.

Shahzil's right leg and left hand are perfect. But it's a hard bony lump in the place of his left foot. Likewise, a similar lump hangs, instead of hand, at the end of his right lower arm. Yet he looks very cute in his layette.

A fortnight elapsed after Eanu's returned to Qatar. Now people gather in Eanu's yard. The day is half bloomed. His wife's cry rises and falls frequently. Two guys arrange chairs under the temporary tarpaulin roof, put up in the yard.

Being Human

"It'll take time to bring Eanukka's body here. I don't think burial is possible today," Eanu's brother informs the surrounding people, pocketing his Smartphone.

Eanu was a middle-aged chain-smoker. Nicotine might be the villain behind his death.

Kayyu stands in distress, following Eanu's demise. Her infant's disability is also a source of perennial pain.

Unwilling to succumb to her tragic fate, Kayyu makes up her mind to live. A mother is the best crutch for a son. She never believes that her disabled son has brought about all the misfortunes.

As misfortune, fortune also comes unexpectedly. Eanu was a prominent figure among the Indians in Qatar. His bosom friends there are very much concerned about Eanu's forlorn family. Their efforts are fruitful. The oil company in Qatar, where Eanu had worked, provides his spouse and son with an enormous financial assistance.

Now Shahzil attempts to get up, though in vain. Each time he feels that he will succeed next time. A strange inner power energizes him. Finally, he stands up with a smile, holding the wooden leg of the cot.

Shahzil finds school a new realm of experience. He stands on his right foot, supported by his left disabled one, and walks with a heavy limp. He wears a special shoe, suitable for the size and shape of his left lump-foot. Some naughty children nickname him. But he is not chagrined.

Monday afternoon, Shahzil stands crestfallen in a nook of the headmaster's room. Another boy, his classmate, with a red cheek and runny nose, wipes his eye with a tissue near the headmaster's table. Shahzil has given the boy a heavy slap across his cheek.

Shahzil has been studying in the eighth standard.

Kayyu hurries to the headmaster's room. Shahzil looks sadly at his mother.

"Why did you slap him?"

"Ma, he called me DUCK."

Unfortunately, the headmaster, a grouchy man, doesn't listen to Shahzil's arguments.

"If you repeat this misbehavior, you cannot continue here," the headmaster admonishes Shazil in front of his mother.

Midsummer holidays. Shahzil has made company with the boys from his neighborhood. They often spend their free time, swimming in the Kanoli canal, when Shahzil keeps their clothes, purses, watches, slings, fishing lines etc., on the bank. As they swim in joy, he watches and imitates them, moving his hands in the air.

At home. The swimming raptures and the whoops from the Kanoli canal echo in Shahzil's mind. He knows well that his mother will never let him swim in the canal. *How I learned computers two years ago?* Shahzil tries to recall. He tamed the mouse first. But typing with one hand was not easy. Yet he succeeded through strenuous efforts.

Lack of one limb will be compensated by the other is a truth.

Shahzil has a sound memory. He recalls things even in his infancy. It was from the air that sense entered his body, he believes. Life was divine and misty in the lap of his mother. Slowly, the sounds got a distinct shape of ideas. Shahzil remembers his mother's cousin Naisa saying, "Why don't you stop breastfeeding, Kayyu? Your child is past two. You had better apply bitter neem paste on your nipple."

Taking a blue bath towel, Shahzil goes to the canal bank. His cronies have already started swimming. He takes off his white T-shirt and black pants. Wearing the bath towel around his waist, he gets down into the canal, and sits in the shallow water, while his friends play in the deep water. He lies on his stomach, his head aloft, and moves his limbs slowly. Seeing this, his friends burst into laughter. "A baby swimmer in the water crib," one of his friends shouts and chortles.

Being Human

"It's a deadly game, Shahzil. If you repeat it, I'll jump into the canal and die," Kayyu warns and threatens her son. She has come to know about her son's adventures in the canal.

Shahzil walks, limping, to the home library, which is full of novels, short stories and romantic and mystic poetry collections, and takes Pearl S. Buck's Letter from Peking. His heart is stirred by passion and love in the novel. He likes romance, though he doesn't have any lover.

It's a balmy morning. Shahzil stealthily goes to practice swimming in the canal. He is no longer a school boy, but a twenty-year-old student engaged in a postgraduate course at St.Thomas College, Thrissur. He wades into the deep water. This time, one of his companions backs him up. Yet he sinks down, salty water touches his throat. He goes on his attempts in vain.

Shahzil gets an appointment order from the Education Department of the State.

"Join now, my boy! You can complete your post-graduation later. It's very difficult to get a government job today," Kayyu advises her son. Shahzil's job and marriage dominate her dream.

It's modern to say, "No dowry". But there's no wedlock without a *gold-lock* on the Kanoli Bank. Contrary to the existing tradition, Shahzil has made up his mind not to accept any dowry. He is handsome, though disabled. It's not impossible to get a bride for a handicapped man. But the best option is to marry from a poor family of many daughters.

Shahzil is more than a peon at the District Educational Office. He is always busy with several creative and useful activities in addition to his official duties. He makes a beautiful vegetable garden in the backyard of his office. Plowing, sowing, watering, weeding...he creates a wonder with one hand and one leg. His colleagues have a very high opinion of him.

Naima comes into Shahzil's life with a bare neck and ears. Her father has gone almost bankrupt, marrying his five daughters off. The dowry system has rocked the boat. Even a coolie bridegroom demands enormous sums of money and gold as dowry.

Naima is slim and fair-skinned. Her eyelashes are darkened with mascara. Her father, who is a truck driver, couldn't provide her with better education because of his meager income. Besides, he thought that investing money in a girl was a waste. There would be no reduction in dowry, even if he educated his daughter well.

Shahzil's philosophy of love is profound. Lovers come from unknown nooks, love, live, and then disappear. He describes love as a multi-faced miracle. Generations come and go. But love remains as the sweetest emotion on the earth.

"Hi sir, don't waste your time staring at me. Get married soon! And enjoy love-wine, sipping," Shahzil advises his forty-year-old colleague.

Sometimes in the evenings, Shahzil and Naima saunter on the grassy canal bank. Water has always been a fascination for him. Now there is a green plastic water pot in his hand. Half-naked, he wades into the water. Holding the water pot upside down within his arm-hand lock, its narrow mouth airtight against water, he floats in the water. Naima fuels him, clapping. He propels his straight body, moving his legs energetically, and then crosses the canal zealously. After a few minutes, he returns with an air of Michael Phelps.

Later, he swims without the water pot, fulfilling a long cherished dream.

Next Saturday. Summer sun will sink in the west soon. Shahzil and Naima are sitting on the grassy canal bank, exposed to the west wind.

"Naima, I've read that life is like a light spreading between the two misty ends. One end is birth, and the other, death. We've no control over these two ends. I find these two edges of human life divine and serene."

"Oh, your words are too heavy!" she stops playing on the WhatsApp and stares at him.

"Naima, do you really love me?"

"Why do you ask me this, dear?"

Being Human

"You're good-looking. But I'm…"

"Really, you're handsome, have a strong mind."

Shahzil puts on his swimming suit. The voice of a white-breasted water-hen vibrates the nearby bamboo thicket. Shahzil dives into the canal with verve. Naima is all smiles.

A strong will and strenuous efforts have turned him into a dauntless swimmer, who swims on under the rainbows and the rain clouds.

Diverse Shades of Insanity

She alights from the midnight train after a jasmine-garland seller. She walks along the pitted road. A large dusty polyethylene bag is swaying from her shoulder. Cars and auto-rickshaws stand in a long row just outside the exit of the railway station. This remote station is bustling only when the trains arrive or depart. Now the vehicles go out with the passengers honking horns. Her dusty figure moves on foot in the dim streetlight, mindless of the hullabaloos made by the taxi drivers and porters. She walks on until the sun in its orange layette looks through the gaps in the canopy of coconut palm leaves on the canal bank.

Some women on the shore stand around their new guest with their arms akimbo, while an old man gazes at her with his thorny eyes. Hearing that an insane woman has come to their village, a stout boy named Sura comes running with his tooth-brush – a white liquid, an amalgam of toothpaste and saliva, dribbles out of his mouth. Soon a human fence is built around her. Everyone eyes her large bag swaying in the lowest branch of a mango tree in the wind. Sun rays begin to produce sweat blobs on the foreheads of the crowd. Rustics return to their homes letting the Kanoli Bank withdraw into its usual silence.

She shouts aloud, sitting for some time on the protruding root of a mango tree. Silence again as though she regains her senses. She watches a black tortoise moving into the bamboo thicket nearby. She runs behind and catches it. Holding it in her left hand, she heaps up yellow and brown mango leaves under the tree with the other hand. She fumbles in her bag and takes out a matchbox with a picture of a peacock on it. She lights the dry leaves with a matchstick. She puts the tortoise in the fire, but it creeps out. She puts it again in the fire. Now the fire is strong. A pungent smell of the burnt tortoise flesh spreads in the west wind. She eats the meat voraciously. Although covered with dust, her countenance has a noble charm.

After her tortoise lunch she sits, leaning against the mango tree, and slowly zones out.

Being Human

She is again enclosed with the human fence by the evening. A crippled boy ventures to imitate her, shouting in the same manner − it seems he has resolved to turn a half-lunatic into a full-lunatic. She is gnashing her teeth. Some rustic guys, who have nothing else to do, enjoy the diverse shades of her insanity.

Her horrible presence helps a mother in feeding her kid, who is reluctant to take food. "Take a little more. Or I'll call that mad woman."

Saru, a coolie woman, who is as nice as pie, observes, and gives some cooked rice with sardine curry to the insane guest. "She's a human being, after all," Saru says.

A balmy afternoon. She looks hale and hearty. Her palms splash the salty water. She swims in the canal. The grime over her body dissolves in the water, and her skin gets back its lost hue. Her voice can be heard far away. She speaks rough Hindi of some remote North Indian village. Now a fisherman's canoe floats by, zigzagging like a snake. He stares at her wet glossy body. Every day, he is seen on the wavelets of the canal. He catches prawns and pearl spot fish with his violet net.

Windy season begins on the Kanoli bank. Night wind brings the smell of the burnt canal fish, along with the fragrance of incense smoldering in the prayer rooms, and the alluring aroma of the jasmine buds blooming on the shore. Diverse smells are always synchronized in the track of the Kanoli wind. This canal was built during the British rule in India. Hundreds of people, most of them coolies, inhabit on this bank.

"Ma, don't you hear the mad woman's shrieks and shouts from the bank now?" Saru's daughter asks, letting out her anxiety on a Monday night.

"Don't worry, my dear. It's windy season. Madness reaches at its top at this time."

The insane woman's shrieks and shouts are thus neglected in the rural logic. Nobody knows that lust has been implanted in her womb.

A midday. The woman roams on the shore in the parching sunlight, when even a crow hesitates to fly. Village folk lose their interest in the newcomer day by day.

A rising sun is creating tiny rainbows on the grass through dew drops. She has just woken up. She communicates with an invisible friend. She makes strange gestures indicative of insanity – guffaws, funny faces, meaningless clinking of her dusty bangles. Often she utters, 'Ma'. Who is her ma? Who is her pa? Did she marry? When did her mind slide from its track? Question waves are thus getting high.

Three months pass since a repulsive lascivious Monday night. She nauseates. Stooping her head, she sits in a huff beside her bivouac for a long time. Her belly swells like a pumpkin. Lust seems a cousin to lunacy. Though lunatic, her behavior is now like that of a typical pregnant lady of the Kanoli bank. She stretches her hand up to pluck an unripe mango from one of the lower branches. It is a seemingly fatigued attempt, yet she gets the mango. She eats it greedily, and then chucks out the tender seed.

After an eight-months noisy stay, she prepares to leave the Kanoli Bank. Taking her precious belongings in the polyethylene bag, she walks slowly as she looks into a void. Nobody dares to stop her. She mutters something in her slangy Hindi. No one can make it out. People watch her sauntering to the tarred road.

Everybody stares at her swollen belly with many dark, bulging questions. She turns and vanishes.

Some rags, dusty papers, and a torn mat piece – like the feathers left behind by the migratory birds – lie scattered under the mango tree on the bank.

Yummy World

Breeze and birds multiply nature's charms. Yet Risha prefers playing online in the living room. The one and only game that Risha likes is **Bakery Story**. Like a figurine, she sits before the tablet.

Yards were once crowded with noisy children. A halcyon past. Nowadays the children rarely play hide-and-seek, elephant-and-mahout, etc. Instead, they withdraw into the secret nooks of the electronic world.

'Yummy World', her dad suggests a name for the bakery, and she likes the name.

Yummy World, though small, is eye-catching. Risha displays dexterity in arranging things. Her chocolate and coffee tables are well-kept and attractive. She has placed the refrigerator, triple-decker, proofing box and kitchen hutch aptly. Really, she doesn't play, but lives in the game. A game is a good experience.

Risha is contented with her new customers in the bakery. *Yummy World fascinates me with a variety of cakes*: one of her visitors writes on the **wall.** There's a delightful collection of carrot cakes, vanilla cupcakes and Black Forest cakes in Yummy World.

Day by day Risha's neighbors in Bakery Story increase. She cogitates about expanding her bakery.

There were just two ovens in the beginning. Later, she bought a deep fryer, a candy oven and a Blue Bun Oven.

Risha's school remains closed, following the COVID-19 pandemic. Bakery Story saves her from drowning in boredom. She never irks her mother, saying 'It's BORING!'

People from diverse cultures join fingers and play the game in the global village.

Risha's mother tongue is Malayalam. Chit-chatting with her neighbors in Bakery Story, she improves her communicative skill in English.

Being Human

Before going to bed, Risha sets food for the customers, who will visit Yummy World in her absence. Like the cakes and cookies, the drinks too are mouth-watering. The spring tea, cappuccino, hot chocolate coffee, mocha, apple tea, eggnog and water melon juice are special attractions in the bakery.

Risha visits Steve's bakery, which spreads over a large area. Being enthralled, Risha requests him to make her one of his neighbors. He is an English man, a stranger to her, like the migratory Siberian crane that just landed in the paddy farm in front of her house. He responds to Risha's request promptly.

"Welcome, my new neighbor! Which gift do you prefer?" Steve says, accepting Risha as his neighbor.

"I prefer cappuccino. Thank you!"

And Steve, the bakery maven, gifts her with cappuccino.

Risha is a ten-year-old svelte girl with a winsome visage. The most brilliant thing about her is that she has been writing a novel. The name of the protagonist in the novel is also Steve. She believes that people with the same names are rather identical in character.

Risha, Steve and others become an effervescent e-community. LMK (let me know) PLMKWC (please let me know when you clear), HAGD (Have a great day!), BTW (by the way) etc., are unique abbreviations in their communication.

I miss you, Steve: somebody has written on the wall in Bakery Story.

What happened to him? Risha ponders about Steve. He is neither her native nor her relative, yet his absence is distressing. A true relationship thrives above creed and color, doesn't find any geographical barrier.

Next day, Risha reads what Steve has written on the wall: *My grandchildren have come. They keep me engaged.* Risha is surprised, realizes that her playmate is an old man.

Steve returns to the game shortly. Risha and others give him a warm welcome.

A week passes through the bakery world.

Unfortunately, Steve is absent again. Risha is afraid that the old man is not likely to be active in the game. Maybe, he is too fatigued to play, or fed up with the game. On mature reflection, she makes up her mind to remove him from the list of her neighbors.

Soon Steve writes to Risha. *Sorry, Yummy World, for being inactive! Unfortunately, I'm not well. Make me your neighbor again, please.*

Risha is a kind girl, who can never rebuff Steve's request. She readily adds him her neighbor. The game continues. Food and consumption are prominent human pleasures.

After a dozen days, one friend writes on the wall: *Hello Steve, where are you?*

Steve replies on the wall: *Hi friends, I'm sick. Please, pray for me.*

Risha is dejected. She visits his bakery frequently, ardently waiting for his return.

After the online class, Risha enters Yummy World, turning on the tablet. Oh, it's upsetting. Her eyes are promptly shuttered against the wall in Bakery Story. Reality is unvarying, even if concealed with a rhino skin. She gazes again. *Steve passed away*: one of his friends or relatives has written it on the wall. Doleful silence lingers in Bakery Story.

"Steve is no more, Dad," Risha feels blue, her moist voice wavers. Her father consoles her. In truth, Steve is a stranger to him. Yet he looks melancholic, as if a genetic mirroring of grief.

Dayal

Dayal's auto rickshaw runs at breakneck speed, rushing through the heat and dust of Chava town. Quite unexpectedly, the rickshaw halts and the jeep behind it diverts to the right, barely avoiding a crash. The jeep driver sticks his head out, yells *"Are you mad, bastard?"*, then drives off.

The rickshaw has run out of fuel. Dayal steps out and takes a can of diesel from behind the back seat. After filling the tank, he continues his journey. He has forgotten hunger and thirst. His mind frequently visits his old house, and always returns with grief and shame.

He had been a clerk under the Irrigation Department. A small family can live comfortably with a clerk's income, yet he had remained bankrupt. He once had a dream – to become the district collector, a glamorous post. Though he tried twice, he failed utterly in the Civil Service Examination. His handwriting, slow and shabby, was the culprit. His father used to say, *when you try to catch an elephant, you will at least find a goat.* Dayal became a clerk. Now, the sorry figure of his father, always struggling to provide, flashes in his mind.

The tarred road ends. Dayal and his auto rickshaw have left the rest of the world behind. They enter a narrow path leading into thick forest as night falls. Crickets slay the silence. Headlights carve a way through the darkness. A deer jumps onto the path, stands and stares at Dayal and his rickshaw, dazzled by the bright light. Dayal waits for it to leave, and continues.

After a while, the vehicle loses its pace and halts with a groan; its wheels are fully immersed in mud. Dayal is too tired to push it out. He puts his head on the handlebar and closes his eyes. Soon, he is asleep.

Sun rays fall through the canopy of leaves, scattering on the front glass of the auto rickshaw, waking Dayal from his dreamless sleep. He gets out of the vehicle, rubbing his eyes and finds a stream. There, he washes his face, then gulps water from the bowl of his palms. The coldness is refreshing.

Being Human

Finished with his morning routine, he goes, sits on a moss-covered stone beneath a huge teak tree. A breeze has started and the branches sway softly, slender as a woman's arms. *There is always a woman behind a man's success*, he thinks. He has read that in some book.

"Behind failure, too," he mutters.

After his father died of liver-cirrhosis, he began shouldering the family's burden all alone. Before long, his mother came down with rheumatism. She could hardly get up anymore, and Dayal had to take over the housework. He loathed cooking. Too late, realizes he how much he has taken his mother for granted.

Now he gets up, stretches. He has made up his mind to explore the forest. Down a narrow path, he spots a reddish-yellow mango lying beneath a wild mango tree. Suddenly he is reminded of his hunger, a clawing thing in his stomach; he picks it up quickly and devours it.

After making his way to the rickshaw, he lies down in the back seat and slips into a nap. When he opens his eyes, standing in front of him is a half-naked tribesman in a dusty dhoti. A bottle of honey dangles in his left hand. A woman, perhaps the man's wife, stands nearby with a bundle of dried twigs on her head.

"Who are you?" The man asks.

Though he is reticent by nature, Dayal decides that he will speak. He tells them who he is, how he came to be here. They grasp human what he is saying, and invite him to their hut. He politely declines. They leave, but not before giving him a match-box.

"How could Simra abandon me?" Dayal settles back into the rickshaw.

Now that she is gone, he understands her at last. She had come from a well-heeled family – a pampered life – with a concept in her mind of a husband, the perfect husband, developed from her love of TV serials and Hindi movies. She longed for a fantasy life, as on the screen, and for a short while after the marriage, she was shy. Her beauty both energized and blinded Dayal. He followed her around like a dog wagging its tail.

"A husband should be a grave man, never a chocolate-boy," his mother reminded him often, and he could not stand her words, her practical wisdom. *She is jealous,* he thought. *Jealous of Simra.* Back then he had been sensitive; his mind and face, pure and young, had captivated his young bride.

They did not have many happy days left. His meager clerk's salary was not enough for her, for all of them. Soon their poverty, and his mother's rheumatism, shattered his wife's long cherished dreams and with it, their romance.

A few months later, his mother passed away. And Simra became a free bird.

Dayal is startled out of his thoughts by a wild, thunderous trumpet. Immediately, he pulls down the drop-down curtains of the auto rickshaw and peeps through a tiny hole between them.

Outside, it is drizzling. Large shapes move in the bush, their footfalls shaking the ground itself; elephants. A grizzled male with long tusks leads the herd. They pass by Dayal and his rickshaw, and through the tangle of grey trunks and stout legs, Dayal sees a baby elephant lumbering along with the rest of them. He stares on, breathless.

Soon, the elephants are gone, disappeared into the depths of the forest. Dayal curls up against the seat, but he cannot sleep. Yesterday's events have risen in his mind and this time, he cannot push them away.

Her father, a churlish middle-aged man, comes by early in the morning. He compels his daughter to take her jewelry, dresses and other belongings. She is poker-faced and obeys her father. Dayal watches all of this, frozen.

"I never thought things would end like this... yours is a wretched birth," her father tells him as they leave.

Being Human

A few minutes later, a black Ambassador car comes to his house with bank and revenue department officials, accompanied by a police jeep. Then start the loan recovery proceedings. Dayal's body and mind burn with humiliation; a large number of villagers have gathered in the yard, watching. Some pity him, while others jeer, laugh, and scold. He cannot find a friendly face.

"We're sorry. We have no other way. The proceedings here are finished," the bank manager tells him. Dayal says nothing. He has lost his house and his land. His pride is steeped in shame. His wife is gone, his neighbors have lost all respect for him, and he misses his mother. There are things more horrible than death in this universe.

The bankers are gone by noon. Dayal takes out a brown leather bag, some clothes, and enters his auto rickshaw, the only thing of value he has left. As he drives, he cannot meet the eyes of the people he passes, the other drivers.

It is as if the whole world is watching, watching and laughing.

The tribal couple leave Dayal cooked tapioca wrapped in banana leaf. They often present him with wild fruits, edible roots, honey and the like. He learns from them how to find bread and soon adopts their ways, their secret philosophy – live today, forget yesterday and neglect tomorrow. The auto rickshaw has become his home. Day by day, his mind convalesces.

Saffron sun peeps through the twigs. Dayal is out for a stroll when he hears an odd noise. Moments later, a car comes nodding its head along the narrow path and stops beside him. A large man steps out, followed by his wife and a four-year-old son.

"I'm Denny, from Chava," the stranger introduces himself. Chava is near his home village, Dayal realizes.

The other man explains. He and his family have lost their way while enjoying the charm of the woods. Dayal nods and points with his index-finger in the right direction out of the forest.

Denny is fazed. "Could you come in a sit until the route is clear for us, please?"

Dayal consents, and gets into the car. Though it is worn-down and untidy, Dayal's remains unerringly polite; life in the wild has not altered his manners.

"Sir" Dayal points to the left. Five meters away, there is a tiger, pausing as it crosses to watch the car.

"Please don't stop, and drive fast, sir."

"What a trip, Dayal! I'd like to come back, without my family, later."

"Everybody likes the forest," says Dayal.

"I'm preparing a research paper on the wildlife here, and I hope… that you can help me with it."

"Yes, with pleasure, sir."

Now they reach the tarred road. "We're out of the forest. You can let me down here, sir."

"O God! I forgot. How do you get back here?" Denny asks. He stops the car. "I intend to come back the day after tomorrow. So if you don't mind, please come with us. You can stay in our outhouse, and show me the way when we return."

Dayal does not decline, as he suspects that otherwise, it will take him many hours of walking to return to his rickshaw.

They drive for a long while. When the car reaches Chava city, Dayal asks Denny to stop the car. "Sir, I'd like to get down here. I would like to see your city and I will wait for you here, the day after tomorrow."

"Very well, I will be here around in the morning… Please, take this." The other man has taken out five hundred rupees and offers it to Dayal.

"No, sir. I cannot."

Being Human

"Take it, please. For being so kind. For food, at least, or whatever else you need."

Dayal takes the currency and bows his head.

After sixteen long years, Dayal saunters along the roads of his home village, the early sun rising and its soft light nostalgic. The village has changed. A movie theater, a wedding-hall, a duplex, a barber's saloon, an English medium school, metal towers and well-furnished shops have appeared, all put up during his long absence. The coconut leaf-thatched huts have been replaced with concrete houses. Nobody calls out at him, and he would hardly recognize himself if he walked by a mirror; a dusty copper colored beard has grown on his face. His body is hairy like a bear. His shirt and pants are faded.

Dayal recognizes one of his old classmates, greets him, *hello!,* but his classmate walks away quickly, avoiding his eyes. Dayal looks down and realizes that he has not washed in some time; he must resemble a tramp.

He continues his walk, a stranger in his own village, where he was born, raised, and lived in for thirty-five years. Yet he wanders with the thrill of a boy at a carnival.

Twilight looms. Dayal is haggard and thirsty. Still he roams, looking around. He halts at a familiar street, enchanted at a two-storied house, an architectural beauty standing by the side of the road. A lady, neither young nor old, sits on the red marble door-step. Her hair is dyed with henna. Dayal walks up, opens the gate, and enters her yard. Up close, his eyes open wide. Sweetness runs through his veins.

She sees him, gets up, and goes into the house. A few minutes later she returns with some coins. She steps up and offers them to him, but he simply gazes at her.

"Simra…"

He has broken the silence. His voice is charcoal, low and rough. Her eyes stare, widen, and glisten… then move away. The moment is ended. She goes back in and slams the door.

Slowly, silently, Dayal turns and leaves, his mind barren, where nothing grows.

Mr. Tension

Google gives several answers to his query, *what causes pain in the left upper arm?* He sticks to heart attack, overlooking all the other causes. Midnight magnifies anxiety, which is intrinsic to his character. His forehead, neck and chest are moist. He finds his spouse and daughter in deep serene sleep. Being in a real tizzy, he lies on his back beside his better half.

A warm flake of sunshine wakes Niyadh up. It's too late in the morning. His routine has been changed since the lockdown began. The fully fledged coronavirus petrifies the world. He's glad that he didn't die in sleep. No pain. Lifting his left arm, he tries to unburden his tension.

Mopping the floor, sweeping the cobwebs, cleaning out the cupboards, rearranging the furniture, weeding in the vegetable garden, burning rubbish in the bonfire… Niyadh and Simna were never conscious of time and trouble during the first three days of the lockdown. Their intrepid daughter was also interested in everything.

Now Niyadh sits at the round sooty table in the kitchen, taking his breakfast.

"Will it raise my blood sugar level?"

"No, dear! A piece of *puttu*[6] and boiled banana won't raise your sugar level. But your habit of eating too much will certainly worsen your condition," Simna warns him in no uncertain terms.

After breakfast, Niyadh saunters to the front yard, accompanied by his eight-year-old daughter, to water plants. Marva is a lean girl with a pleasant visage. It's not noon, yet the sun is scorching. No rain clouds. Summer rain is a distant possibility. The water level in their well declines significantly, signaling a drought. The climate has transformed like the new generation. In Niyadh's view, the modern summer is drought, and the monsoon, flood.

---

[6] *A breakfast dish (steamed rice flour mixed with shredded coconut).*

Being Human

Marva stares at the kingfisher perching on the coconut leaf near the well, while Niyadh finishes watering plants at full tilt. It's too hot to stand in the open air. They come in post-haste, and then watch TV in the drawing room. News channels abound with pandemic reports. As in the previous night, Niyadh feels an instantaneous pain in his left arm. He takes his smartphone and googles further for the reason. It's deep-rooted in his thought that he has some fatal cardiac problem. He turns gloomy. Just then Simna comes from the kitchen with banana fritters. Soon she cracks jokes. Marva guffaws. But Niyadh is muted. She's inured to her husband's unbridled tension. She has even coined a nickname for him – 'Mr. Tension'.

He has been more vulnerable to tensions since he was diagnosed a diabetic. Sometimes he seems dim-witted, albeit he's a lecturer in economics at Sree Krishna College, Guruvayur. He always longs for longevity.

Oh! He wasted a muscular body, which I wish I had, Niyadh intones while going through a newspaper report about a young man's suicide.

The lockdown continues. Roads of life have either been blocked or narrowed. Niyadh's arm pain doesn't abate. He goes on exploring more medical websites. A harrowing report catches his attention. It was about a lady, who had continuous arm pain for a fortnight. Consequently, she died of a heart attack. She was a chain-smoker, whereas he was neither a smoker nor a drunkard. He neglects the fact that the lady had chest pain too.

The tall tufted Niyadh counts days, *seven more days maximum!*

Am I really afraid of death? No, never. Isn't it an eternal sleep free from all the fret and fever? Will I be reborn? Will the clarion sound for gathering before the Creator? Anyway, death seems a beauty in mystery. Yet I don't want to die. How can my wife and daughter live without me? They will be exposed in this callous world. Who will play elephant-and-mahout with my sweet Marva? Yesterday, when I was about to go out, she begs, "Dad, please stay at home! Police will arrest you for breaking the lockdown law, I'm afraid." Yes, they truly need me. Niyadh ponders over his death and its aftermath. He finds that the thought of leaving one's dearest people and precious belongings turns death doleful and dreadful.

A couple of months ago, Niyadh went to the Diagnostic Service Center in the city for a complete health check-up. Everything was normal, except his heart rate of 103 beats per minute. Moments of titanic tension. Another ECG reading was taken the next day. He prayed to the Invisible Universal Power, his God. Still his heart rate was more than 100 bpm.

"ECG is normal, though the heart rate is high. Your blood pressure should be taken care of. So, come again after ten days for monitoring your BP," Dr. Rinson advised him.

Niyadh returned home with a turbulent mind. He sat in an armchair in the drawing room. Simna came so close to him that her breast touched his tuft of hair. She knew his mood very well. She skimmed off the scum of his tension and let his mind cool. Slowly, romance sprouted from solace. A vehement love zigzagged swallowing all his tensions.

That tranquility prevailed in Niyadh's mind for ten days. Most of the patients were weary. A stout boy sneezed, waking up a fragile wrinkled woman from her lethargic nap. Niyadh, too, sat patiently. Really, he was in a tizzy. As his turn came, he entered in and sat beside the doctor.

"It's still 140/90. And you're already diabetic. So, you had better take medicine for BP," the doctor prescribed Starpress-XL 25.

At home.

Do I really have high BP? Or is it merely a by-product of my anxiety? Niyadh was in a quandary. Succumbing to his wife's insistence, he took the beta blocker capsule Starpress-XL 25. And he kept calm. At twilight, he dipped into the website of Starpress-XL and found the side effects of the medicine. A platoon of tension marched through the corridor of his mind. The next morning, he felt chest pain and almost all the other side effects he had read. Without consulting with the doctor, he himself adjusted the dose as half a capsule daily. He bought an Omron Blood Pressure Monitor. He found that his blood pressure level was normal most of the time. Ultimately, he stopped dawdling and made up his mind to stop taking medicine for BP.

Being Human

Niyadh's mind emerged out of anxiety clouds. He amused his wife and daughter with his unusual ability to create jokes from the then situation. Life bloomed like Neelakurnji in their living room.

But that elation was short-lived. Another chest pain, though a mild one, brought about new tension waves. He googled again for the reason. He read, *Stopping Starpress XL medicine suddenly will increase heart rate, and may even lead to heart attack.* And that sketchy information pushed him into a chasm of death-fear.

Niyadh had become insomniac. Soon he went to his doctor, and disclosed everything, including why he stopped Starpress-XL. Dr. Rinson comforted him and prescribed an alternative medicine Telmiget 20.

"Are you OK now? When will the next heart attack come?" Simna asks with a smile. Marva chortles.

"Unless you feed your mind with something positive, it will feed on something negative," Simna reminded her husband.

Niyadh regained his lost tranquility.

The lockdown continues. Niyadh enjoys the drizzle outside from his balcony. In a jiffy, the bright sunshine falls, creating tiny rainbows in the droplets of water on the banana leaves in the yard.

Suddenly, he feels pain again in his left arm. His enjoyment of nature disappears behind the wild anxieties. *Stopping Starpress XL medicine suddenly will increase heart rate, and may even lead to heart attack,* he recalls his website reading and whispers to himself. He also remembers a fortnight-long arm pain of the lady and her consequent death of heart attack. He has to leave his family forever shortly, he cogitates rubbing his arm.

Niyadh recalls his childhood companion's Facebook post on the eve of his demise following a cardiac arrest. The friend has written, *Not certain whether I will get sleep if I go to bed. Not certain whether I will get up if I sleep. This life is worthless as a rag.* Niyadh firmly believes that his friend had made out symptoms of cardiac arrest before death caught him, yet he was unwilling to consult with a cardiologist. Maybe it was due to his laziness or financial difficulties.

Ultimately, Niyadh decides to go to hospital for a detailed medical check-up. Simna also supports his decision. But it's not easy to travel in the present situation. He is likely to be stopped and questioned on the way by police. An affidavit detailing the purpose of the journey is mandatory. The lockdown rules are very rigid. Yet he isn't ready to recoil from his resolve, for life and peace are so precious. He wishes Simna and Marva could accompany him, but it's risky. Wearing a mask, he sets out alone.

The doctor gets a clear picture of Niyadh's unbridled psychological stress from his words and countenance.

"ECG is normal, Niyadh. HR 110 may be due to your anxieties. Don't worry. If you want further clarification, a TMT may be conducted."

"Doctor, I'm ready to undergo the TMT," Niyadh, who was skeptical about the ECG reading, agrees without reluctance.

After the TMT, the cardiologist patted Niyadh consolingly on the shoulder.

"Your heart functions well, Niyadh. Continue medicines for diabetes and BP."

The Everest of tension is pulverized in Niyadh's mind.

"Thank you, doctor! When I feel pain in my arm or chest, I conclude that it's due to heart attack."

"Personally, I too feel so," the doctor utters with a smile.

Black And White Spectacles

Dilyab is searching for his father's death certificate in a faded green iron box in the storeroom. Quite surprisingly, he finds the spectacles – a rare inheritance from his father. As he takes it, a cockroach, which was clinging to its thick frame, falls down. He looks through its thick glasses – sees his father. And an aching memory fills in his eyes.

Then he couldn't listen to his father's words. Perhaps he was deafened by the prospect of a distant rapture. Or he longed for peace amidst his secret tension.

His father Zainu owned a printing press, which was the sole source of his family's income. But the monsoon always rocked the boat. Diverse cultural and art programs faltered to a stop – nobody came to his press to print the program notices and receipt books. People curled themselves up in their houses with the laziness of a cat while it rained cats and dogs. Though he was on the verge of bankruptcy, his father never tried to borrow money from others, for his inherited nobility made him scrupulous. Noble births grow in poverty as the chaff burns.

"I didn't get a single coin today. It's very difficult to go forward like this." As Zainu had expressed his helplessness, his wife and son kept silent, unwilling to bother about their uprooting issue. Zainu had a mind that was always moist – very conducive too – for the rich growth of tension. He had become a diabetic patient – sugar syrup flowed through his veins, rusting his internal engines. He struggled hard to satisfy the basic needs of his family. But his wife Saya was not sensible enough – and his son not matured enough – to realize his efforts. The root always remained unnoticed beneath the stem and bloom.

Saya came to Zainu's life with an acre of coconut grove, another acre of paddy farm, and a mound of gold. But she was an illiterate woman, the youngest of the four daughters of a rich widow residing in the next village. Though the dowry dazzled him, he couldn't foresee the squabbles in store for him. Dilyab had learned from his parents how marriage could knit the day and the night together. His dad and mom became the most matchless couple in the universe, and he a compound word, made up of his father's softness and knowledge and his mother's coarseness and ignorance.

"Look at my left leg, Dil. There's a swelling near my ankle. I feel burning pain inside." Zainu eyed Dilyab packing his luggage silently.

"Don't worry, Dad. Please apply Betadine ointment there. It'll be healed soon."

"Where're you going?"

"Dad, I'm going on a pleasure trip to Ooty along with my colleagues. I'll come back day after tomorrow."

Zainu had struggled hard to provide his son with a better education. He covered his poverty with a smile. It was a matter of wonder how he fulfilled his son's needs even in the midst of bankruptcy. Dilyab graduated in education from the Kerala University. Before too long, he was appointed as an English teacher at CWA English Higher Secondary School, Karikad. Though he got a meager salary from the school, it was really a buttress to his family. He was fortunate to get a couple of good colleagues at school.

Hearing a horn honking, he said, "Dad, my friends are waiting outside. Bye."

"When you reach there, don't forget to call me. Be very careful..."

Zainu noticed a red hue spreading rapidly around the affected area on his leg, with a burning pain and consequent uneasiness. It was a diabetic swelling. After a couple of days, all the joys that had been deposited in Dilyab's mind by the pleasure trip were shattered before his father's leg. He took his dad to Koja Hospital in the city. A minor surgery was suggested. A junior surgeon came to room no.203, where Zainu was admitted, followed by a nurse, who held a tray with a few scissors, knives, a bottle of lotion, another bottle of surgical spirit, some cotton, and so on.

The doctor performed a minor surgery on his leg and dressed the wound.

"You'd regularly bring him here for dressing the wound," Dr.Paul advised Dilyab.

The doctor removed the puss with fragments of flesh from the sore on Zainu's leg on alternative days. Healing the wound was very difficult in his diabetic body.

He fell into a chasm of silence. Betadine, a yellow ointment, and a thick piece of cotton hid a horrible hole in his leg. He lay on his bed like a broken winged pigeon. He grew thin, and his penury thick, day by day. He couldn't even get up to shave; silver bristles thrived on his chin.

His wife was trying to pour rice porridge into his mouth with a steel spoon. Aching wound had turned him peppery. He didn't feel hungry. He had lost the sense of taste. "Take it away, Saya. I don't want it."

He pushed his wife's hand with the spoon, which fell down – rice porridge lay scattered on the mosaic floor. That kind of behavior was quite unexpected from him.

Dilyab soothed his dad with mild words, and ultimately tamed his rage. He sat beside him, holding his palm. Then he noticed tears filling up in his father's eyes.

A cloudy morning. Hearing Saya's shriek, their neighbors came like moths. Kakka brought a phial of honey, for whom honey was the panacea for every disease. Zainu used to share his pains and pleasures with Kakka, an aged lean neighbor. Kakka poured the honey into his friend's mouth. Zainu was lying on his bed with a faint gleam of consciousness, breathing unusually and noisily. An ambulance came nodding its head along the country road. Dilyab took his father to the ambulance with the assistance of two stout young men.

Deep silence prevailed in the ICU of Koja Hospital. He stared at his father through a tiny glass window on the door. A duty nurse opened the door and asked him to talk with the doctor in the ICU.

"How's my dad, sir?" Dilyab inquired in a doleful tone.

"He's in a coma state. Now you call him aloud."

He went to his father's bed and called him, "Dad...dad...DAD..."

Being Human

He noticed – he alone noticed – a teardrop in the corner of his father's closed eye. That was his dad's last teardrop like a seal on the container containing all the pain he had experienced during his lifetime.

Saya sat curled up on the damp floor of the dining room amidst the holy showers, fenced by her friends and relatives.

Dark night and the snow of December gobbled everything. There were no friends and relatives, except his mother and an aunt, in Dilyab's house after his father's funeral. Emptiness deepened in his heart. He couldn't resist an impulse. Secretly he took his dad's unwashed cotton shirt from a black hanger – brought it close to his nose – got the smell of his dad's sweat mixed with the jasmine scent.

That trip to Ooty remains as a stain in his mind even after ten years. He rears himself – his immature mind – for not taking his dad to the doctor in time. Perhaps that wouldn't have made any difference. But it is a fact that an early treatment often avoids the complication in a diabetic patient. People often fail to do the right thing at the right time, he contemplates. And he wipes the dust from his dad's spectacles with the end of his white dhoti.

The Cowboy

There were always shrubs, shades, and mysteries on the face of Peringadam, the two acres of land owned by my grandmother. I shaved a part of that large face, put up a house.

I had seen used condoms lying among the shrubs, like the remnants of some secret romance, where my bedroom stands now.

My grandmother's cowshed was exactly at where my bedroom is. Grandma's black cow with white stripes and the cowboy shared the darkness, smell of dung, and mosquitoes in the cowshed. The cowboy was not at all bothered about the poor surroundings, for a deep love always lingered in the attic of his soul.

More than a cowboy, he assisted my grandmother in all the domestic duties. He never said, 'No' to her, even when he was dog-tired. He was human to the core.

One morning, grandma was shocked…shrieked. All rushed to the cowshed. It was tragic. The cowboy was lying dead in the cowshed.

An unnatural death. The neighboring folk believed that the cowboy was killed by a ghost.

After a sumptuous lunch, my wife and I are snoozing in our bedroom. Suddenly, I wake up – my spouse too – hearing echoes of a forlorn voice, which I'm unable to define in words. In truth, I had heard the same voice before.

As my wife admits that she also heard such a sound, I'm pretty sure that what I've experienced is not an auditory hallucination. *Then, what's this voice?* Maybe, another mystery in the mysterious universe! Or, perhaps, the voice of the cowboy from the old cowshed. He had died with the suppressed dreams. *Died or killed?* Possibly, he was murdered for loving a girl from the upper class.

Being Human

My wife slips into the snooze again. Many truths had been buried in the graves of the world. I lose my sleep among the smoldering thoughts.

Yiyo

A whining rises above the pit-a-pat of rain.

"Don't you hear that sound, Dad?"

"Put the pillow over your ear, and sleep well, my darling."

The animal-whining and the wind-howling continue. Rain bathes the night.

Darkness melts away in the dawn light. The hair-raising sounds of the previous night still echo in Kanishma's mind. She opens her bedroom window, looks at the fresh face of the day. There is a puddle in the yard waiting to be dried in sunlight. The wet sand has been carpeted with fallen leaves, green and yellow. A bunch of brown coconuts lie scattered. Frogs croak, mistaking the summer rain for monsoon rain.

Soon her eyes catch a puppy, sooty in hue, under the eaves of her house.

"Poor thing!" falls from her lips.

"Dad, please come. See a puppy down the window!"

The puppy is in a tight spot, his eyes communicate. It's distinct that he needs food and shelter.

Yadhu goes to the puppy, with his daughter Kanishma following closely behind. He is a mason with limestone-like physique and fruity psyche. He takes the puppy in his hand, pats him on the crest.

"How did this puppy come here, Dad?"

"Perhaps, his mother brought him here, finding a shelter under the eaves. It'd been raining all night."

"Then, where's his mother?'

"The dam may be wandering for food somewhere."

Yadhu rounds his lips like the snout of a pig, producing a squeak to catch the attention of the puppy.

Being Human

Kanishma touches her new friend with wonder. She calls him 'Yiyo'. She doesn't know the meaning of this name. Though *Yiyo* is not in her vernacular tongue, she likes it for its auditory charm.

The traces of trauma slowly vanish from Yiyo's eyes. Soon he becomes a member in Kanishma's family. Human-canine bonding is thousands of years old.

Kanishma's dolls are discarded in the nook of her bedroom. For a child, a real live playmate is more important. She enters his heart, feeding him with boiled rice, sardine heads, chicken pieces… He is a voracious eater.

Yiyo gets love and care of Kanishma's parents as well. They permit him inside the house. When Kanishma reads Stevenson's Treasure Island, Yiyo sits on the tiled floor, brooding.

Kanishma beautifies Yiyo, combing his fur. She applies Cuticura talcum powder to his skin, and then polishes his nails. With a merry mien, he lets her antics on his body.

"Yiyo is growing fast. Certainly, I don't dislike him. But I can't let him sleep inside our house, especially at night", Kanishma's mother opens her mind.

"You're right. We want his service outside at night." Yadhu finds a night watchman in Yiyo.

One murky midnight in October, not only Kanishma's family, but their neighbors also wake up, hearing Yiyo's loud bark. His eyes shine in the dark. He is no longer a puppy.

The people don't come out, fearing an ambush. Instead, they shoot sharp lights from their torches. The light-arrows create an abstract art on the black canvass of night.

Now Yiyo stops his barking. He pants heavily, staring into the dark.

Next morning, Kanishma's mother is sweeping the yard. She finds paw prints, not a dog's, in the sand.

Yadhu stands with arms akimbo, gaping at the paw prints.

Now his neighbors stand around the paw prints. They reach a conclusion that a tiger came there last night. So Yiyo barked continuously.

The Forest Department officials visit Yadhu's yard in the afternoon. They confirm the tiger's presence in the area, examining the paw prints.

How did the tiger come there? This is a distinct question with an indistinct answer.

There is a tea shop on the roadside within the walking distance of Kanishma's home. Weary drivers from the distant states stop their trucks near the tea shop to take lime tea and snacks, and refresh themselves. They reach here at night, driving along forest roads. So there is a possibility for a tiger to leap into one of these opens trucks, hide among the goods, and alight here as the vehicle comes to a halt.

The shadows of fright fall over the whole village. Even then, what comforts Kanishma is the valorous presence of Yiyo. She believes that Yiyo frightened the tiger yesterday. Yiyo becomes her true hero.

Next day, the tiger is trapped by the Forest Department. People come in large numbers to see the tiger prancing in the iron-barred cage. Kanishma calls on the ferocious guest of their village, along with Yiyo. Now that Yiyo loses his temper before the tiger, she takes him back home quickly.

January 10, 2020.

Yadhu and his wife enter their portico in the gloaming. They have bought a Red Velvet Cake from a bakery in the town. The front door of the house is open. Yiyo is fast asleep beside a flowerpot. A tiny piece of dark chocolate lies close to his right foreleg.

Yadhu puts the cake on the dining table.

"Kanishma… Where're you, darling?" Yadhu raises his voice. But no response.

12th Wedding Anniversary Mr. & Mrs. Yadhu is visible in black letters on the cake.

Being Human

They search for their daughter.

"Where's Kanishma?" Yadhu asks Yiyo.

Finding Yiyo's death-like sleep, Yadhu suspects a tragic happening. *Who brought the dark chocolate here? Is it a sedative chocolate? What happened to my daughter?*

Soon the police arrive. Their dog sniffs, and then runs to the copse on the riverbank, not far away from Kanishma's house. The police and locals follow the dog with torches. They search through the night chill in the copse, but in vain.

Sun logs a new day. Waking up from his long sleep, Yiyo hurries to Kanishma's bedroom, where her mother sits propped against the pillows. She broods about her daughter. Yiyo steps out of human-canine silence.

Kanishma's photo with the caption *MISSING* goes viral on social networks. Her winsome face, with a red ornamental dot in the center of the forehead, wets the eyes of the world. People pray for her safe return.

Yiyo goes to the copse, sniffing. There are leeches lurking for blood in the copse. He stands among the trees, throwing his eyes into the river. He spends the whole night here.

9 A.M.

Yiyo darts like a bullet train, carrying a mind full of pangs. His destination is Kanishma's home. Hearing his loud bark, Yadhu comes out of the house. Yiyo barks unusually, turning back frequently.

Yiyo is fretful. Again, he walks to the riverbank, barking, turning back… Yadhu follows him. His nephew is willing to accompany him into the copse. Yiyo stops beside a fallen tree – its trunk on the land, and its branches in the river. He jumps onto the trunk and barks, looking towards the branches. An empty hemp sack hangs on the root-wad of the tree.

Yadhu crumples up in grief. His nephew holds him tight, consoles him. Kanishma's bloated body lies upside down among branches of the fallen tree. The corpse has begun to rot – the right ear is eaten by fish.

The police file a first information report (FIR). They suspect sexual assault on the girl before the murder. The culprit might have given the sedative chocolate to both Kanishma and Yiyo. Maybe, she was suffocated within his lecherous hands. He might have flung the dead body into the river, bringing it in the sack.

Really Kanishma's body was found by Yiyo's keen senses. The police and people admire Yiyo's brilliance. He comes into the limelight.

The smell of cremation lingers in the air. An everlasting emptiness spreads in Yadhu's house.

Now the full moon wipes off darkness. Yadhu hears Yiyo's howling from the copse. His voice is not down in the mouth. Sixth sense is a beautiful reality beyond the murky mysteries in the universe.

The New Highway

What seems insignificant for many may be significant for one. Naisa is delighted at the sight. She planted this mango tree five years ago. Now it blooms, causing euphoric waves to pass through her veins. Bringing her nose close to the bunch of blooms, she inhales the fragrance of earth. Soon a sad thought perturbs her.

The mango tree will be an aching memory before too long. The new highway will be constructed, burying paddy fields and mangroves. It will devour ponds with fishes and frogs, drive away birds with sweet twittering. Trees will be uprooted. Mighty legs of the new bridge will choke the Kanoli canal.

The new highway is the need of the time – everybody, except the victims of the land acquisition, says in no uncertain terms. Officers with sense and sensitivity must be entrusted with the task of preparing the alignment and acquiring the land for the highway, otherwise the whole procedure will be an inhuman drama. Any development destroying nature is defective.

Sitting in the veranda, Naisa watches the paddy field in front of her house. The field is parched as her mind. Though the harvest is over, Eenam Club is not likely to conduct the Annual Celebrations this year. Almost all men in Naisa's locality, which is known as Peringadam, are members of Eenam Club.

Every year, Eenam club organized various cultural programs. They put up a temporary stage in the field after the harvest, using the areca nut palm trunks, bamboo poles, coconut leaves, tarpaulin, and coir rope. The stage was embellished with lights, colorful silk clothes, papers, and balloons. Either a drama or a musical concert was performed before a large crowd. In addition to that, there were various artistic performances by the girls and boys in the locality. As the moon bloomed in the sky, the rustics transformed joyous, forgetting their hunger and miseries in the artistic fervor.

It was during one such festival that Naisa met her better half. Thousands of eyes had been scattered in the field, yet his eyes magnetized her through the moon-man-made lights. He was selling bangles, his face and colorful bangles gleamed in the festival night. Her thoughts stretched towards him through the sweet vibes.

Love began to burgeon. He zigzagged in her valley beneath the hanging mangoes.

Naisa's mind returns from the romantic valley fifty years away.

The land acquisition procedures are in the final stage. The paddy field with its nostalgic rhythms will be gobbled shortly by the new highway.

Though living a frugal life, she is contented at home. Eight coconut palms stand like sentinels around her house, her income comes from the coconuts.

Where do I go? This is the recurring question in Naisa's mind.

The last day blooms in her yard. Carrying a cloth bag, Naisa comes out of her house. A woman police constable leads her into the police van. Naisa is a wizened woman, bent like a question mark. Her face resembles a cauliflower. Just before stepping into the police van, she turns back to look at her house – the last wet glance.

"Let me live in my sand", Naisa implores the rubber-eared police woman, raising her shivering voice. She curses the corrupt officials, who have altered the original alignment of the proposed highway to make a killing, satisfying the land mafia, and only because of that, she has to leave her house now. The land mafias foresee a Himalayan hike in the value of the land on both sides of the proposed highway.

The police have been deployed in the area. The air is turbulent with the protest slogans against the land acquisition and eviction. "Where do we go?" the impecunious inhabitants ask. Their question is answered by another question by the Deputy Collector, "Don't you want development?" In fact, both these questions reach nowhere.

Naisa's bank account has been credited with the compensation. But the question is how she will, or who will, build a house for her. She is old, too feeble to manage her things. Not merely money, thoughts and efforts are also required for building a house, even if a small one.

She has been alone in her house since her husband's death seven years ago. She lost her husband in the festival in the next village. He had gone there for selling bangles and toys. The temple yard was crowded. Ten caparisoned elephants stood in a raw. Sorrows and sufferings of the people vanish in the music from a variety of instruments, both the traditional and the modern. Even the ill-famed rural ruffian stood tamed in the music. The elephants moved their ears rhythmically. Soon the fireworks display started. The mahouts were drunk with the musical delight, dazzled by the brilliance of the fireworks. Quite unexpectedly, one of the elephants turned violent, trumpeting, perhaps due to the excessive humidity or the scary sound that each firework produced. It turned and dashed, breaking chains in its legs. People scattered. Music ended in shrieks. Tragically, Naisa's husband Quasim was succumbed to death under the giant foot of the elephant. A child was also trampled to death. Several people were injured. An auto rickshaw was mangled. The elephant turned a Swift car upside down, trampled two motor scooters, uprooted a dozen banana plants... Finally, the Elephant Squad came and shot the elephant with a tranquilizer gun.

But nobody could tranquilize Naisa.

Fragrant memory often surfaced, scuba-diving through her loneliness. Hallucination was sometimes a boon to her. She conversed with her husband. Words fell down from her shriveled lips without voice.

Naisa has a distant relative, who lives in a flat in the nearest city. He often invites her to stay with his family. Now that she doesn't like city life, she turns down his invitation. Moreover, an old guest's presence won't always be welcome in that flat. How can she leave her house, where her husband's love and smell linger?

The police drop Naisa on the roadside, give her a false promise that they will find her a home shortly. The police van moves with the other protesters. Emaciated, Naisa walks to an old peepal tree. She puts the cloth bag down under the canopy of leaves, sits on the sand, cogitating about her plight.

A cool wind blows. Heat of the day dissolves in the night chill. Naisa bundles her up in an old taupe woolen blanket. She is enticed by the fireflies, but she cannot make out whether they are flying in her mind or among gliricidia plants.

Tomorrow, vehicles will swish along the new highway, but no traveler will remember Naisa.

Tomorrow, the news media will bring her miseries to the public notice. Consequently, she will be given shelter in some old age home, where she will have to live as a prisoner, with her likes and dreams incarcerated.

About the Author

Fabiyas M V is a writer from Orumanayur village in Kerala, India. He is the author of *Monsoon Turbulence* (Poetry Nook, United States), *Shelter within the Peanut Shells* (Red Cherry Books, India), Kanoli *Kaleidoscope* (PunksWritePoemsPress, United States), *Eternal Fragments* (Erbacce Press, UK), *Stringless Lives* (Budding Light Press, Australia), *Moonlight and Solitude* (Raspberry Books, India).

His fiction and poetry have appeared in several anthologies, magazines, and journals. Westerly (Western Australian University), British Council, Hawaii Review (University of Hawaii), Red Coyote (University of South Dakota), Noctua Review (Southern Connecticut State University), Rathalla Review (Rosemont College), Event (Douglas College), Forward Poetry, Off the Coast, Silver Blade, Pear Tree Press, Poetry Nook, Zoetic Press, Zimbell House Publishing, Typehouse, Structo, Encircle Publications, Lumpen, Shooter, Nous, Evening Street Review, The Curlew, Alban Lake, Verbal Art, Tower Poetry, Chiltern Arts, Anima, Of Nepalese Clay, Malevolent Soap, Qommunicate Publishing, the Elephant, BFP Books, Slice Of The Moon Books, Stillpoint Magazine, Kansas City Voices, Portmanteau, Pendle War Poetry and Creative Writing Ink are some of his publishers.

He has won many international accolades including Merseyside at War Poetry Award from Liverpool University; Lest We Forget Poetry Prize from Auckland War Memorial Museum; and Animal Poetry Prize 2012 from RSPCA (Royal Society for Prevention of Cruelties against Animals, UK). He was the finalist for Global Poetry Prize 2015 by the United Poets Laureate International (UPLI) in Vienna. His poems have been broadcast on All India Radio. Poetry Nook and The Literary Hatchet have nominated him for the Pushcart Prize.

He has been working as a teacher in English at Gov. Higher Secondary School, Maranchery in Kerala.

His spouse is Ajina, and daughters are Mehna and Isha.

www.ingramcontent.com/pod-product-compliance
Lightning Source LLC
Chambersburg PA
CBHW070313120726
47910CB00007B/2472